FLY IN THE OINTMENT

FLY IN THE OINTMENT

ANNE FINE

LARGE PRINT

Oxford

Copyright © Anne Fine, 2008

First published in Great Britain 2008
by
Bantam Press
an imprint of Transworld Publishers

Published in Large Print 2008 by ISIS Publishing Ltd.,
7 Centremead, Osney Mead, Oxford OX2 0ES
by arrangement with
Transworld Publishers
A Random House Group Company

British Library Cataloguing in Publication Data
Fine, Anne
    Fly in the ointment. – Large print ed.
    1. Large type books
    I. Title
    823.9'14 [F]

    ISBN 978–0–7531–8102–7 (hb)
    ISBN 978–0–7531–8103–4 (pb)

Printed and bound in Great Britain by
T. J. International Ltd., Padstow, Cornwall

CHAPTER
ONE

I get it all the time now, from everyone, even the Governor.

"Exemplary behaviour, Lois. No one can fault you on that. And Mrs McKay doesn't like to think what she will do without you when it comes to the accounts."

She taps the pile of reports and looks at me over her half-moon specs as I wait for the "only one fly" bit.

"Only one fly in the ointment, and that's the fact that you still won't face up to your guilt."

Guilt, though — that's in the eye of the beholder. And it isn't as if I'm still pretending that I wasn't there and didn't do a thing. I kept that line up through the trial, of course. But that was only because I thought there was a chance I'd get away with it. (So did my lawyer — reasonable doubt and all that.) But afterwards I never kept pretending. I'd simply explain the circumstances and say to people, "Well, tell me what you think you'd have done. *You* be the judge."

In any case, guilt isn't minted fresh. Each story's triggered by some sort of accident and littered with others all along the way. A chance meeting here. A run of bad luck there. "Go back and write it down," says Mrs Kuperschmidt, whenever she visits. "That's bound

1

to make you think more deeply about the choices you made. You'll come to see you could have done things differently. Then, when you next come up before the board, you will be able to convince them that you've made headway. They can take a chance on letting you back in the community."

"Community" indeed! I'm trying not to curl my lip, but if the famous so-called community that we're supposed to have around us had offered even a spot of help along the way at times I needed it, I wouldn't have ended up here. I don't say that to Mrs Kuperschmidt, of course. I simply nod and ask her for more notepads and pencils. I will set it down. Though how far back I have to start is quite a mystery. The only certainty is that it couldn't possibly have happened if Larry hadn't been born. And that leads back to my son Malachy. And that leads back to Stuart, and I can't think what made me want to marry *him*. It caused enough trouble. Even the night before my wedding, Dad was still giving it me with both barrels. "When I think back on all our hopes for you. You realize there's still time to change your mind."

"But I don't *want* to change it."

"Lois, you make your bed and you will have to lie in it. Don't think you can come crying back here when you see the mistake you've made."

"Don't think for a moment I will!"

The tin-pot dictator never hidden deep inside him must have taken my sticking up for myself as a massive affront, because he didn't show up for the wedding. Simply didn't show up! I don't have brothers or sisters.

2

(My parents' other two babies had been stillborn.) And my only really good friend had just gone off to work in South Carolina. So on my side it was about the sparsest gathering of people you can imagine. No chance of failing to notice that my own father wasn't there.

In the foyer, I caught my mother's arm. "It's almost *time*. Where *is* he?"

She cringed. (She was good at that.) "I'm not really sure, dear."

I was ready to shake her. "Mum! This is my *wedding*. Where *is* he? He can't still be parking the car. What's going *on*?"

She fiddled with the cuffs of her new suit. "I'm sorry, dear. He just said something about not wanting to watch you toss your life away on —"

She stopped.

In gathering disgust, I let go of her sleeve. "On —?"

"Well, I suppose, on Stuart really, dear."

"Oh," I said, still smarting from the previous night. "You mean 'that pipsqueak trainee insurance salesman from down the street'?"

My mother cleared her face of all expression.

I changed tack. "So what did *you* say?"

She turned resentful, as if she felt that she of all people was blameless.

"Mu-um!" I wailed (as quietly as I could, for fear of being overheard by the two colleagues Stuart had invited at the last minute to swell the numbers). "You must have said *something*. Surely you told Dad he had no right to spoil my wedding day. Surely you told him —"

My mother never cared for criticism. "Well, Lois, if you feel I've let you down so badly, perhaps you'd rather that I wasn't here either."

I stood there, speechless. Just then a woman appeared in the Registry Office doorway. "The marriage of Lois Cartright and Stuart Henderson. Please step inside now."

Blind to the unfolding drama, Stuart left his widowed mother and came over to join me. I didn't know what to do so I took his arm. We walked into the big airy office awash with flowers, and took our places in front of the massive desk. The others trooped in behind us. I can't recall a thing that happened or a word that was said. Only one thought was hammering in my brain through the whole ceremony: had my mother come in behind us? I wasn't going to humiliate myself by turning to look, and yet I couldn't think of anything else. If paying attention at your wedding is any part of the deal at all, we can't have been married properly. But still the Registrar declared us man and wife, and even as Stuart took up her suggestion and kissed me, I was peeking over his shoulder, looking for Mum.

She wasn't there. I was so *hurt*. You can imagine. I felt my parents had behaved appallingly. I'm not sure how I got through the next couple of hours, and when at last there was some time to think about it afterwards, my anger boiled over. They had gone too far — both of them. If they thought they could make up for this in a hurry, then they were wrong. I didn't care how long it was before we spoke again. That was their problem, not mine. I certainly wasn't going to make any effort to get in contact.

The days turned into weeks. I stayed firm, even though there were a couple of occasions when, but for the rift between us, I might have rushed home sobbing. Stuart turned out to be a whole lot less loving than I'd hoped. I had mistaken his lack of inner fire for manly gentleness. And, like most women, I'd all too charitably taken his unwillingness ever to interrupt me or take a different line on anything for companionable agreement whereas in fact, of course, more often than not his lack of response stemmed from simple indifference.

The vague unease that maybe Dad had shown a whole lot better judgement than I'd thought was probably another reason why I never went back to patch up the quarrel between us. But after a while things took their own course. Stuart's own mother — his only real relation in the world — died of a heart attack. My parents were perfectly well aware how close the two of them had been, and still they sent no card. (I knew they knew.) So in revenge I didn't get in touch when, only a few weeks after my mother-in-law's lonely little funeral, I became pregnant. Or when I lost that baby. Or when, a year or so later, I finally found myself pregnant again.

It was exactly five months after that, at one of my clinic check-ups, that someone I half remembered from school tapped at a page of the paper she'd taken off the waiting-room table, and passed it across to me.

I glanced down amiably enough. "What am I supposed to be looking at?"

She pointed.

It was one of those black-edged squares on the back page. A death announcement. One of our teachers? Maybe even someone our own age?

I had to read it twice before I grasped it. "Isobel Mary Cartright? But that's my *mother*."

I must have gone bone white. She gave me a curious glance. "Didn't you know?"

I shook my head, and barely whispered, "No."

She thought I meant about the announcement. "Oh, well," she said. "Maybe one of your mother's friends offered to phone it in, and your dad forgot to mention it."

"No, no!" I couldn't help wailing. "You don't understand. I didn't *know*."

If she'd been startled before, now she was staring. "How could you not know about your own mother's *death*?"

I felt my cheeks burn as I studied the words for the third time. "*Beloved wife of Ronald*." Nothing about me. I can remember thinking I ought to explain. Then suddenly everything round me was bleached of colour — shimmeringly bright — and things went blurry. Perhaps I nearly fainted. Certainly without any talk about who was next in line, somebody ushered me through a door and on to a chair in one of the cubicles. And there I sat until a doctor came and fussed about whether she could get a proper blood-pressure reading or whether I'd have to come back. I'm sure she hadn't grasped I'd only just that minute learned of my mother's death. The paper I was clutching was almost a week old. I think she probably assumed that catching sight of that announcement of a funeral I must have so recently attended had sent me into some fresh surge of grief.

I drove home in a daze of shock and misery. All afternoon my mind was racing, but I couldn't manage one clear thought. I kept trying to ring Stuart, but he wasn't answering and the firm's switchboard kept up the usual barrage of defence: "I don't think he's back from lunch yet." "I'm afraid he hasn't picked up his messages." "I think he might be out of the office this afternoon."

So I just waited. When he finally walked through the door I more or less *ordered* him to pick up the phone and ring my father. He gave one of his martyred sighs and, just as he always did whenever I asked him to phone some tradesman to complain about sloppy work or an outrageous bill, he said he couldn't do it if I was standing there listening to every word. So, knowing even at the start that he would make as shoddy a job of the call as he always does when plumbers or electricians are concerned, I went out in the garden and watched through the window until he put down the phone.

I hurried back. "Well? What did he say?"

The very speed of my return made Stuart prickly. "Not very much."

I was in no mood to take things gently. "What do you mean, 'Not very much'?"

"Just that. Not much."

"But did he *explain*?"

"Explain?"

I lost patience. "For God's sake, Stuart! Did he explain why I had to read about my own mother's death and funeral by chance in the *paper*?"

I could tell from his scowl that Stuart was really resentful about being stuck in the middle of all this unpleasantness.

"*Well?*" I persisted.

And, would you believe it, my own husband pitched in against me! Choosing the tone of voice you'd use on a petulant child, he told me, "Well, Lois, he did say he couldn't see what else you could reasonably have expected."

I could barely believe what I was hearing. "Sorry?"

"Well, you know. Given that you had quarrelled with the two of them, and never rang . . ."

"I quarrelled with *them*? *I* never rang? I like that! Surely you had the guts to remind Dad that it was *them* who ruined our wedding — him by not showing up and her by getting in a snit and taking off. Surely you at least mentioned that!"

Now he'd turned sullen. "Lois, if you're so sure you're in the right about all this, maybe you should have made the call yourself."

"*If* I'm so sure? Aren't *you*? After all, it was your wedding day as well as mine."

He shrugged. "All water under the bridge now, though, isn't it? So what's the point of going on about it?"

I do believe that was the closest I ever came to hitting Stuart. I do remember thinking, "One battle at a time," and as good as dismissing him. I slid my hand over my churning baby. What if I lost this one too, and purely out of temper? I forced myself to wait till I was firmly back under control. Then I picked up the phone and rang my father's number, as I knew he had known I would.

I stuck right in. Without a word of greeting, I challenged him. "In the paper it said Mum died 'after a brave fight'. Does that mean she had cancer?"

"Oh, hello Lois." He sounded almost smug. "Yes. That's right. It started in her stomach a year ago last Christmas, and ended up all over."

I tried to stick to a tone of icy control. "And why wasn't I told?"

His answer astonished me. "Well, Lois, that's the way your mother wanted it."

"She *told* you not to tell me?"

"That's right."

I must have sounded like a howling eight-year-old. "But *why*?"

I'll swear the smug tinge to his tone deepened to one of pleasure. Clearly this was the moment the two of them had been waiting for through all those hospital appointments and blood tests, recurrences and relapses, and the last slide downhill. I'm sure that, after Mum's death, my father even thought it was a real pity his sick wife couldn't have defied the natural order of things sufficiently to relish the moment properly along with him.

"What your mother actually said, Lois, was that she didn't think that you'd be interested."

"*What?*"

"Be fair. You hadn't bothered with us from the day you married. No calls. No visits. You couldn't have made it clearer that, now you'd got Stuart, the two of us were just a couple of cast-offs. And so your mother —"

I'm sure he might have carried on for hours, spinning the story his way. But I'd put down the phone.

Stuart was back in the room and looking at me. "See, Lois? I *told* you that there was no point."

And, try as I might, I could not fail to recognize the exact same hatefully smug tone of voice I'd just been hearing from my father.

CHAPTER
TWO

Is that the moment when my heart iced over? I was still far too young to realize the truth — that more people than you'd think walk round with no real care or concern for anyone else on earth. If I'd known that, I could have saved myself by feeling pity for whatever it was that tipped all three of them — my father, my mother and even my own ill-chosen husband — out in the world with such ungenerous souls. I could have felt compassion for what was missing in them, and simply gone upstairs and packed my bags. I could have found some drab flat I could just about afford, and raised my child alone, blaming the three of them for the fact that I had to see the poor mite off each morning to a series of childminders or some dismal nursery.

Or I could freeze my heart. Numb all real feeling. Make sure that everything was paralysed, except for the last few impulses I'd need to make enough excuses for the man I'd married to keep our lives rolling along. Just as in childhood I'd managed to ignore the looks of irritation on my father's face whenever I popped my head up under his evening paper, so, as an adult, I could learn to brush aside my husband's indifference. After all, hadn't I been warned? You make your bed and you must lie on it. If it turned out to be a bed of nails, then I could do the same as other disappointed wives — cushion the pain with pillows of womanly invention: "Oh, men are *hopeless* on the phone", "Boys grow up with such different skills", "You simply can't expect a bloke to understand that sort of thing."

So that's what I did. I look back now and I'm astonished at the effort I must have put in over the years to tell myself things weren't that bad. I clutched at hints of unhappiness in other marriages. I relished the company of women whose husbands' failings seemed far worse than Stuart's. I think if I'd lived on a street of wife-beaters, gamblers and drunks, I would have spent my whole life pushing Malachy's stroller back and forth past all their garden gates, flattering myself that I'd made an excellent choice (or maybe, in less robust moments, assuring myself that, if I had not drawn my particular marital short straw, I would have drawn some other). I was a far cry from the woman I'd have been if I had had the sense to listen to my father, or, like so many others, put off the wedding long enough to see whether, in time, attraction soured into disgust and pity into irritation.

Or grave good looks into the constant absence of a smile. For Stuart turned out to be grumpy. Not even the nice sort of grumpy, as when a man sinks comfortably into the depths of the sofa and grouses amiably about the perfidy of the government or the shortness of his daughters' skirts. No. Mean-spirited grumpy. Over the years Stuart must have got round to criticizing every single thing about me: my parenting

12

skills, my dress sense, my cooking — even my spelling. He was the sort of person you'd move away from at a party, and I was so stupid and green that all I ever did was try even harder to please him.

Well, more fool me. The only way to get through to people like Stuart is to bring a frying pan down on their heads, along with a sharp command to "Stop that now!" I just went quiet and thought I was doing the right thing by staying. ("A baby needs his father.") Once there's a child, of course, few women have the energy to deal with larger problems. And so our deadly marriage dragged on for years. Most people know the score: those days of letting the words you think of saying to break the silence echo in test runs through your brain before you decide not to bother; those nights of sleeping poorly for fear of letting an unguarded leg cross the cool gap between the two of you and be mistaken for a gesture of remorse. Gradually you find that the life you'd hoped to share has been divided into "spheres of influence". Separate development, really. People are right. If you're afraid of loneliness, then don't for heaven's sake make the mistake of getting married.

But Malachy was a joy. There's something so *hopeful* about babies, toddlers, small children. A whole new life just waiting to be unzipped. He was the happiest of boys through all his primary schooling. I blame that secondary school for what went wrong. How do these teachers manage to close their eyes to all that bullying? The wrong sort of clothes, or family, or face? Disaster! The wrong sort of personality? Tough luck on you.

You'll simply have to put up with a heap of vicious shoving and hitting all the way to school in the morning, through every break-time, and all the way home at night. Small wonder so many schoolchildren bunk off, turn inwards or take to comforts like drugs. I think my Malachy had less strength of will than most. (I'd hate to think that he was under even more pressure.) And I didn't have the sense to march up to the school and take him out of there, giving those teachers a taste of the truth: "Why should I leave my son with you? He's neither safe nor happy, and what little you teach him is not worth the misery of staying all day to learn it. Forget the whole deal."

So, for whatever reason — and this is my bitterest regret — I didn't do it. And by fifteen my son was probably a hopeless case. A terrible thing to say. Fifteen? Lost cause? Of course I didn't know it at the time. Believe the comforts people offer you and you can easily manage to persuade yourself that everyone else's teenagers look as sour and pale and moody as Malachy did, spend whole days in bed, and steal from their parents' pockets. Who is to know the shade of difference between healthy rebellion and the slow, steady disintegration of a young person's personality?

Not Stuart. He put a huge amount of effort into staying away from the house. We barely saw him. Meetings. Work trips. Conferences abroad. And not me, either. I only saw what I was brave enough to see, and that was no more than what I felt strong enough to deal with. I only worked part-time (in a dry-cleaner's — perhaps the fumes softened my brain). But they were long enough hours to offer the escape from truth so many parents need.

Now, of course, all this time later, I can face the facts. Already by fourteen Malachy was in with the bad crowd. By fifteen he was in thrall to drugs. By sixteen he was a junkie — dishonest and snivelling, with a heap of seedy friends who, even when you'd taken Malachy's phone away from him, still managed to find some way of signalling this week's special offer to him over the hedge.

Did we talk about it, Stuart and I? Barely at all, beyond the day-to-day recounting of our son's tantrums and disappearances, occasional paranoid fits and the anxious complaints of the neighbours. I certainly wouldn't have asked for Stuart's help or advice, knowing only too well the sort of wrangle it would have set in train. More of his tiresome accusations: "If you'd not spoiled that boy . . ." My counter-arguments: "If you had ever been *here*." No. Better to press on alone, phoning the police to insist that they came round to clear the drug-sellers away from the front of our house; making excuses to drop Malachy off so close to school in the morning that there'd be at least a chance he'd feel too idle even to bunk off; trying to stop him leaving the house for ludicrously spurious reasons at all times of the day and night.

All hopeless. And, once Malachy had finally rubbed enough of his reeling brain cells together to spark the realization that he was now old enough to leave school, a whole lot worse. I dreaded leaving the house. I dreaded coming home again. And I loathed being in it. So when the social worker, Mrs Kuperschmidt, finally advised me to offer him the choice — full drug rehabilitation in a clinic or leave the house — he sulked, then shouted, but he left the house. The next time I saw him he was hanging round the door to the shopping centre along with a girl with a nose jewel so lurid it looked like a bad sore, and shorts halfway up her arse.

I stopped to talk to him. "Look at you, Malachy. Just *look* at you."

He turned away. "Oh, piss off, Mum!"

A spark of interest flashed across the girl's bland face. "Are you Mally's mother?"

To this day I am glad I held back the bitter "I *used* to be" that sprang to mind and told the girl instead, "Yes, I'm his mother. And on the day he finally manages to convince me he's sorted himself out, then I'll be happy to have him back."

She turned to Malachy. "Did you hear what she said?"

He muttered sourly at the pavement slabs beneath his feet.

"*Well?*" she demanded.

He scowled at her. "Well, what?"

"What are you going to *do?*"

He looked a bit baffled. "What do you mean?"

"I'm asking, are you going back?"

He nodded towards me. "What, with her?"

"Yes."

He stared at me with venom. "Not if she's going to keep on and on at me like before. Not if she's going to be rude to my friends and nag me all the time."

Oh, blessed are the peacemakers. She turned to me. "Well, *are* you?"

"What, going to keep on at him and shoo off his druggy friends?"

"Yes."

"Well, yes I am," I said. "He can come home, but only when he's finished with whatever crap it is he's ruining his life with now."

"Oh, right," she said.

And that was that. Frankly, I couldn't see why she hadn't grasped it first time around, unless she was blasted, or her brains had been rotted by glue fumes. I went into the shopping centre and got the things I needed, along with four big fat juicy and expensive sandwiches and two large bottles of peach and mango juice — Malachy's favourite — to hand over on my way out.

But they were gone, with only a couple of cigarette ends rolling about in the draught from the doors to show that they'd ever been there. I drove home rather too fast, in some distress about my son and irritation at the wasted expense of the food I had bought them.

If I am honest, it was probably only because this extra shopping was on my mind — could I perhaps pass the beef and mustard sandwich off, with a salad, as Stuart's supper? — that I even noticed that my husband had gone.

Yes, gone. And not just with the jacket he'd have taken with him in case it turned chilly later, but with his long black coat. Curious, I looked in the cupboard under the stairs. His boots weren't there — only the running shoes I'd bought after Stuart's ticking-off at his last routine check-up for not taking any exercise, shoes he'd neither wanted nor worn.

I went to the desk we'd built in under the stairs. At first glance it looked as cluttered as usual. But when I studied what was lying about I noticed it was only paperwork to do with the house. Directories. Bills. Receipts. Nothing of Stuart's and, most unusually, nothing at all to do with his work.

I opened the drawers. One looked suspiciously empty. I tried a sort of test, rooting through for his driving licence or passport — any paperwork to do with Stuart.

Nothing to be found.

I went upstairs, and into the bedroom we shared. I opened the closet to see a couple of suits he never wore, a few shirts that he hated, and shoes I'd bought him that he had always complained felt as uncomfortable as walking round in cardboard boxes. I pulled out a drawer to find a pair of golfing socks I'd meant to send to Oxfam, a heap of handkerchiefs, and one or two of those sorts of weird little leather straps that are something to do with wearing trousers with braces.

I looked in the pretty raffia bin. Right at the bottom, under a heap of smeary tissues I had dropped in there, he'd shoved a crumpled paper bag. I opened it and found a couple of foil-wrapped condoms he'd clearly

18

tidied out of the back of the drawer while he was packing, and dropped in there to save me (and him) unnecessary embarrassment.

The shame of it! I sat on the bed and watched my face go beetroot in the mirror. To have a husband leave, and not even notice! When had the bloody man gone? It couldn't have been that morning. There hadn't been the time. The day before, while I was working? Or could it even have been the day before that? I was so used to paying no attention to Stuart's comings and goings, his calls to say that things were running late, his talk of cancelled trains and nights in the city. No doubt before he bought that microwave oven (for my birthday!) I might have had some vested interest in actually listening to his excuses and his explanations. These days I tended only to mutter "What a shame" and "How annoying for you" and hope that the call would be over before *The Archers*.

I finally worked it out. It must have been the day before, because when I'd come home from work there'd been a note from Stuart on the table letting me know that Martin Tallentire from next door had come round to borrow our ladder yet again.

But since then, nothing.

I wondered if I should phone him at the office. Then irritation rose. Why bloody should I? If the man proved to be such a mean pig that he could choose to do a flit without the courtesy of a single word, then let him. I was so furious I strode around the house picking up droppings from our eighteen-year marriage and putting them in bin bags. Then I sat at the table and ate the cheese and celery sandwich (I'd thought the girl might be a vegetarian), and thought things over.

Try as I might to suffer the flood of worries I thought a person ought to feel in circumstances like mine, only two thoughts kept surfacing. The first was that I couldn't stay at the dry-cleaner's. Much as I liked the job, I knew I couldn't depend on Stuart to fund me for much longer. Even if he changed his mind and came back tomorrow, I couldn't be sure he'd stay. If I was going to keep a roof over my head, I'd have to brush up my accounting skills and get a proper job.

The second thought was how very stupid the two of us had been not to split years ago.

My only actual *feeling* was relief.

CHAPTER
THREE

The feeling lasted. Not just for the rest of the afternoon (and through the next sandwich) but through the long quiet evening. In a symbolic gesture of "good riddance" I put fresh sheets on the bed and took off the downie Stuart had hogged so often, leaving me shivering. Instead, I put on the cotton blankets that I preferred, and could peel off and pull back over again, as my own body demanded.

Spread like a starfish, I fell asleep in moments. At twelve I jack-knifed upright, fearful that Stuart might have lain awake in his hotel room (or in his lover's bed — who was to guess?) and changed his mind. I pictured him sliding out from under the covers, pulling his clothes on and getting some taxi-driver to drop him at the end of our street. I even imagined his footsteps coming up the path, his key scraping the lock.

And then I thought, "No, damn it! You can't walk out without a word and come back just as you choose." I hurried down the stairs to run the bolt across the front door. (The back is always bolted.) "Just try to get in now!" I warned him as I went back to bed and then, astonishingly, slept through till morning.

I woke with the sense that this was all some unimagined gift. I had been given a second chance to live my own life, not the one I'd twisted out of shape trying to fit in with Stuart. The light shone brighter on the walls. The birdsong sounded merrier. Even my tea tasted better. I dressed with care in case Stuart popped into the dry-cleaner's to tell me he was in love, or off to Thailand, or whatever. I got in early enough to warn Soraya I would soon be handing in my notice, but not so early that she had time to prise much out of me before we were engulfed by the first rush of customers dropping things off on the way to their own jobs.

I kept hearing singing all day. Yes, it was really like that. I'd hear a voice cheerfully carolling through some upbeat song and look up, startled beyond belief to find it was my own. I swapped sandwiches with Brenda at lunch time even though I hate tuna. I think that I was on a perfect cloud of happiness.

Till I saw Malachy. He was hanging around in a doorway across the street, obviously hoping to catch me. I felt the usual shaft of irritation that my son's days were so empty he could start loitering at three for something that wasn't going to happen before five-thirty. But that is druggies for you. And watching him shuffle round aimlessly did at least remind me why Mrs Kuperschmidt and I had finally toughened up. I saw the stains on his jacket and thought of the countless times I'd had to kneel to clean up his dribbles and vomit. I looked at his filthy haystack hair and my head swam with memories of those perpetual arguments about bathing and changing. I looked at his

22

hands rooting nervously in the depths of his pockets and thought of how often they'd filched money from mine.

But the longer he stood there, the harder it would be to deny him whatever he wanted. And maybe he had brought a message from his father. So in the end I left Soraya holding the fort, and crossed the street. "Hello, Malachy."

"Hi, Mum."

"Feeling all right?"

"Bit groggy," he admitted. He trawled through what little was left of his brain for proper manners. "How are you?"

"I'm fine," I told him brightly. "Have you seen your father?"

"No," he said, looking behind him anxiously. "Why? Is he here?"

"Not just this minute," I assured him. "I was just wondering if he had looked you up at all in the last couple of days."

I couldn't tell from Malachy's blank look if he was even trying to remember. I pushed a little harder. "So you haven't seen him recently? No news? No notes or letters?"

"No." Out of sheer habit he started to forge excuses for failing to live up to what he took to be some expectation of mine. "But I've been moving about a bit . . ."

"Oh, yes?" I recalled Mrs Kuperschmidt warning me not to appear too curious about his life on the streets. ("It shades all too easily into seeming to sympathize with a choice that he's making for himself.") But I did try one question. "What, with that nice girl?"

"Which nice girl?"

"You know." I touched the side of my nose. "The one with the red jewel here."

"Oh, her." He shrugged. "No, she's gone now."

"What, home?" (More fool me.)

"London."

"Oh, dear." I felt the old heart-sinking chill. There is no fighting this demon. Certainly no winning, even for girls who mean well. Unwisely pushing Mrs Kuperschmidt's strictures aside, I asked my son, "And what about you?"

Down came the scowl like a shutter. "What *about* me?"

It all came back in force. The screaming and the tears. The hammering on doors at two in the morning. The brazen deceit and petty thievery. The angry phone calls from other parents. The visits from police and meetings with social workers.

Never again. Mrs Kuperschmidt was right to have helped me make the decision crystal clear to him: stay clean, or stay out. I nodded back towards the dry-cleaner's. "I'd better be getting back."

He shook his head like a dog scrambling out of water. I wondered if he was trying to rattle his brain into some different pattern in which his reason for showing up would become clear to him again. If so, it worked. "Mum, can you lend me some money?"

It was another of Mrs Kuperschmidt's rules, but still I broke it. While I was rooting in my purse, I told him

24

reproachfully, "I bought you and that girl two really nice sandwiches yesterday, but by the time I came out of the supermarket, you had already gone."

"Yesterday?"

He clearly hadn't the faintest memory. I tipped more money into his grubby hand than he expected and, while he was still hunched over, greedily counting it, I hurried off back to my own life.

CHAPTER
FOUR

Who would have thought a husband of nearly twenty years could vanish with so little fuss? For days on end I went round waiting for the phone to ring. Nothing. I have my pride. I didn't want to be the one to make the call. I would have scoured his letters for clues but not a single envelope that bore his name fell on the mat.

That set alarm bells ringing. He'd left the paperwork to do with the house, the mortgage loan and the utilities. But I defy any woman to sit alone night after night, however contentedly, and not think about her future. After a week I borrowed Soraya's mobile to ring his. I had intended to break off the call as soon as he answered, but all I heard was a recorded voice: "This number is no longer in service."

Furious with myself for even wanting to know about a man who was behaving so badly, I rang his office number. A strange voice answered. I didn't say who I was. "I think I might have the wrong extension number," I said. "I'm looking for Stuart Henderson."

"Stuart? He's left."

"Left? You mean, for the day? Or left the job?"

"No longer with the firm. He left over a month ago now." The voice sharpened professionally. "Is it a matter I can deal with for you?"

"No, no. Can you just tell me where he's gone?"

"I've no idea. You could try the people upstairs. Extension 317. They might be able to help you."

They might, but wouldn't, of course. "Data Protection Act . . . previous employee's privacy . . . blah, blah . . . blah, blah." And, to be fair, I didn't humiliate myself by saying who I was, just asked, "Well, is the last address you have for him the one that I have here? 12 Rosslyn Road?"

There was a pause, and then the man said, "Well, since you know it already I suppose there's no harm in saying that's where we've sent on a few things, and nothing's come back yet."

But nothing had come to me. So. No precipitous decision. No sudden brainstorm. No rush of despair. Stuart had clearly planned his bunk far enough ahead to get his mail successfully redirected. All that evening I raged and fretted. How *dare* he? How dare he take it upon himself alone to call time on a marriage as lengthy as ours — slide off without a word, leaving me with a house I only half owned, accounts under his name, and all the rest of the legalities to do with living?

Next day, a Power of Attorney came.

It was a stiff fat thing. I had to read it twice before I realized Stuart had legally deputed me to deal with everything to do with the house and all we owned. Clutching it as carefully as if it were my own reprieve, I took it in to work and when one of the solicitors on the corner came in to collect her blouses, shoved it towards her.

"Can I do *anything*? Even sell the house?"

She ran her fingers over some of the chunks of lardy legal prose and settled on others. Then she raised her head. "Your husband ought to find himself a far more careful legal adviser. The way this thing's been drawn up, you can sell anything you like, including the house. And there's nothing to stop you from keeping every penny."

Old habits die so hard. I actually heard myself defending my louse of a husband. "Oh, I'm sure that's what he wanted. Just for convenience." And I was sure it was. Just for a moment I'd wondered if he planned to go abroad for ever, or even walk into the sea. But it was far more likely that Stuart — careful and fastidious as he was — had weighed up the relative merits of leaving me with a legally stalled life, or with the endless tangles of a fair division, or with everything, and chosen the last. In some men, generosity would have been the spur. In Stuart it would be selfishness, pure and simple. He'd find it less of a bother to go to Ikea and buy a new bed and chairs and towels than face me over a table and explain.

The next few weeks were happy, happy, happy. It is *exhilarating* to be shot of a man whose every word or look drags down your spirits. I painted the bathroom the yellow he'd thought was "probably too yellow". I threw out the monstrous chest of drawers his mother left us and he felt we ought to keep "out of respect". I stopped even thinking in terms of what Stuart always

28

used to call "a proper meal" and took to eating exactly what I fancied when I was hungry. (And I lost six pounds.) I moved the television upstairs, and took to my bed as early as I chose, eating crackers and cheese with lime pickle and not thinking twice about stains on my nightie. If true contentment is living free from irritation, then I was content.

Everyone at work put my good spirits down to the fact that I was leaving. "But, Lois, what are you going to *do*? You can't stop work at your age!" I didn't like to tell them that way back in early youth I'd taken the trouble to qualify myself for a far better job than standing behind a counter tutting over stains. On my last day, I brought in a lavish cake. They had good-luck cards to give me. And though there'd been much talk of the four of us going out for a celebratory drink together after SwiftClean closed, Soraya avoided bars, Brenda was off, and Ravij felt he really ought to stay on the premises a few minutes longer in case the repairman he'd been waiting for all day finally showed up.

At twenty to six, I kissed Soraya and Ravij goodbye and strolled to the bus stop. Two drunks were sitting on the bench and one was spitting. Repelled, I walked on past. I wasn't in a hurry. By the next bus stop I was in my stride, so kept on walking. It was a lovely soft evening. I went through Queen's Park, along the canalside walk the council had smartened up at huge expense, and up on to the old stone bridge.

Hearing a barney starting up somewhere below me, I rested my arms on the cool gritty parapet and leaned over to look. On the towpath beneath, a tarty-looking young woman was ripping into some unfortunate still out of sight under the arch. Her face was twisted with temper. Her arms kept lashing out towards whoever it was who'd sparked her fury. The accusations ricocheted up. "Stupid! . . . Already *warned* you." Each time she hurled herself forward I'd hear her choked and incoherent shrieks echoing over and again under the archway. "Offering crap like that to Wilbur! . . . Wilbur! . . . Wilbur! . . . Want to get us *mashed . . . mashed . . . mashed . . . ?* You fool! . . . fool! . . . fool!"

The arms kept flailing. The girl was in such a tantrum she could have been trying to push whoever it was who had made her so furious into the river. Was it because the sheer frustration fuelling her rage brought back so many memories of scenes with Malachy that I suddenly thought, "My God! That could be some poor child that she's attacking!" And I leaned over the bridge as far as I dared, to check on the victim.

It was my own son.

CHAPTER
FIVE

I followed them at least a mile along the canal path. The young woman kept on screeching. I was too far behind to get the gist of it, but it was clear that she was one of those people on whom anger works like a pump. Each step she took, she sounded louder and shriller.

Suddenly she parked herself down on a bench. I hurried to hide behind some huge and hideous sign detailing the natural beauties to be seen across the water. The sign was made in sections, like a dressing-table mirror, and through the gaps I watched the furious young woman toss back her raggedy hair and light a cigarette. It must have done something to calm her because after a moment my Malachy dared put out a hand to ask for his share of it. He pulled a couple of deep drags down into his own lungs and the two of them stayed there, seemingly without speaking, until she tossed the cigarette away and they set off again. The stub was still leaking its thin acrid trail when I trod over it a moment later.

At the next bridge they climbed the steps to the road. I walked past the shops on the other side, keeping behind till they suddenly parked themselves on a bench by a bus stop. At once I darted into a place called Body and Soul and wandered round among the essences and lotions, keeping my eye on them through the shop window until a bus drew up between us.

When it moved off, the two of them had vanished.

I hurried out to check the number on the back. 18A. Forth Hill and Danbury — neither of them estates on which you'd want to hang about. I watched the bus sail over the rise and vanish. It had been a shock to see my son take that sort of abuse — even from a young woman as angry as this one — and not fight back. He'd always seemed to know how to defend himself when he'd had grief from me.

But then again, he wouldn't be the first man in the world to think that if he was having sex with a woman he was obliged to put up with almost anything. *Could* he be sleeping with her? She had looked noticeably older than him, but that could be at least in part due to her harshly dyed hair. In her grotesquely garish shoes she'd looked a bit of a slag, and it was hard to imagine Malachy climbing into bed and actually *wanting* her. But then again, he wasn't much of a catch himself. Over the last couple of years his skin had worsened and he'd started slumping. The drugs had drained the freshness out of him until at times he looked, even to his mother, a bit like a teenage pensioner.

That night I did what I had promised myself I'd never have to do again, and phoned Mrs Kuperschmidt. She did her best to console me. Her wash of statistics swept on, but only into one ear and straight out of the other, for there was nothing about Malachy to give me reason to believe he might be one of the lucky ones she kept on mentioning who would bounce back again some day, as right as rain.

But I was comforted by her insistence that there was nothing I could do. "And, Lois, never forget that there are *degrees* of losing a child. Right now, you and Stuart must be at about your lowest ebb with Malachy."

You and Stuart? I realized suddenly I hadn't mentioned he had left the house. For some daft reason it seemed important to finish the call before she cottoned on and started to attribute my son's freshly destructive surge to recent strains in our marriage. Instantly I stopped trawling for comfort and tried to convince her that she'd done the business. "Sarah, I know you're right. I suppose I simply needed to hear it one more time from a professional. Malachy's the only one who can deal with his problem."

"That's right. Until he actually asks for help —"

We parted with the old remembered flurries of "Thanks so much" and "Any time at all". I put the phone down. Almost at once it rang again and, thinking that one last snippet of advice might have occurred to Mrs Kuperschmidt, I felt obliged to answer.

A voice so rough that I could barely make out the words snarled a threat. "You tell that fucking son of yours that Wilbur wants his money. *Now.*"

All the old terrors flooded back. I slammed the phone down. It rang again. I picked it up. Before the viper at the other end could spit out a single word, I shouted, "Just you listen to me! My son hasn't lived here for *months*. I don't even know where he is. So don't ring this number again."

I slammed down the phone. It rang again and again, till I unplugged it. Of course I couldn't sleep. At three in the morning, making a pot of tea, I plugged the phone back in its socket. Less than an hour later its shrill insistent ring began again. God help me, this time, as I pulled the plug out of the socket, I thought back to the scene under the bridge and wished with all my heart that Malachy's tarty and vile-tempered companion had put her body weight behind the hitting business properly, and pushed that little bastard, my own son, in the canal to drown.

CHAPTER
SIX

And so began a week of jumping at shadows, sensing footsteps behind me wherever I went, and noticing every car that stayed behind me for more than a single turning. I caught men's eyes in the street and felt cold waves of paranoia. Could this be some friend of Wilbur's? Even Wilbur himself?

On Saturday night I looked out to see a scruffy young man leaning against the fence across the street, staring my way. Without stopping to think, I rang the local police for the first time since I'd thrown Malachy out. They took the usual age to answer, and the desk officer wasted another half a minute introducing himself before starting his bored litany.

"So do you recognize this person you say is watching your house?"

"No."

"Has he knocked on your door?"

"No."

"Made no approaches at all?"

"Well, no. He's just sort of standing there in a threatening fashion. You see, just over a week ago —"

But PC Wood wasn't interested in what had happened a week ago. "Is this man carrying a weapon?"

I lost my patience. "How am *I* supposed to know? And if he is, he'd surely have more sense than to wave it about on a suburban street!"

There came the trained pause as I was given a couple of moments to collect myself. I waited for the next question, but by then PC Wood had evidently taken the opportunity of the short break to reckon he'd put in enough of the groundwork to move on to excuses. "The thing is, Mrs Henderson, we're rather short-staffed at the moment. You see, Saturday's a busy night. So before we pull one of our patrol cars away from the usual troublespots —"

"You mean, interrupt your mates eating chips in some quiet lay-by?"

"I beg your pardon?"

I dropped a finger to cut off the call before I lost my temper. The scruffy young man was still watching the house. I looked at my watch. Eight-thirty. There might be hours more of this — another sleepless night.

I rang the Tallentires next door. Their teenage daughter Tansy picked up the phone. "For heaven's *sake*! I'm *com* — Oh. Hi, Lois."

"Tansy, I'm after a quick favour."

She was already being interrupted by a voice in the background. "Is that Lois? Tell her I'll have that ladder back to them first thing in the morning."

For just a second I wondered if her father's choice of phrasing — "back to *them*" — was born of tact, or cheering confirmation that I wasn't the only person to fail to notice my husband had walked out. But the lout on the street was still glowering my way in an

36

intimidating fashion, so I came back to the matter at hand. "Tansy, could you and your dad come out and watch my back for me while I clear off some nasty piece of work who's standing across the street, trying to threaten me?"

Not even giving her the chance to plead some gripping moment in their favourite soap, I put down the phone, flung open my front door and stormed out towards my tormentor.

"You haven't long," I warned. "The police are on their way. I just want to tell you that if I ever see you on this street again I'll get a stalking order slapped on you. And don't bother with any more of the threatening calls either, because as from tonight my phone will be on a police trace."

Even before I'd finished, Tansy had come up behind. "Lois —"

The young man turned towards her. "What the *fuck*?"

I felt a hand on my shoulder. It was Tansy's father. "Lois —"

I shook it off. "No, really, Martin. I'm fine. I'm simply making it clear to this young man that I never want to see or hear from him again. His sordid druggy affairs are nothing to do with me."

"My *what*?" Again the young man turned to Tansy. "For God's sake! Tell the stupid cow that I don't even *smoke*."

Martin's hand was back on my shoulder. "Lois, I really do think —"

Only then did I realize. "Oh, God! Is he just standing here waiting to go out with Tansy?" I turned back. "Oh, I am sorry. I was quite sure you were a drug-dealer."

"Well, thanks a bunch!"

"I'm sorry, Lois," Martin said. His look was one of deepest sympathy. "I never realized Malachy was back with you."

"He's not!" I snapped. "I just assumed this fellow thought he was."

Nobody spoke after that. I think they all thought I'd taken leave of my senses. After a moment Tansy turned back to the house, presumably to finish her primping. Taking no chances, her boyfriend promptly followed. Once they were safely inside, I found Martin steering me firmly back up the path towards my own doorway. "Goodnight, Lois."

"Goodnight, Martin. Sorry. I'm really, really sorry. Thanks for being so nice about it."

"That's all right, Lois. Better get back in, though. Isn't that your phone?"

I went inside and crumpled. On my slide down to the floor I glowered at the wedding photo I'd lifted down on my first Stuart-cleansing trawl but then put back because the little pale patch on the wall had so annoyed me. This time there would be no reprieve. Each careless glance its way was a reminder that my husband had taken advantage of *for better*, then let me down when Malachy and his druggy entourage had turned our life together into *for worse*.

I'm finished too, now. I found myself thinking the words as clearly as if I'd spoken them aloud. If we had married in church, I might well have agreed to stick with you for richer, for poorer and even in sickness and in health. But no one in her right mind would promise to stick things out through silence and deception.

The phone cut off, then started to ring again. Still, I felt stronger, knowing that first thing on Monday morning I'd start proceedings for divorce. It meant I'd have to deal with the terrifying fall-out from Malachy's indebtedness all by myself. But when had Stuart ever been a help with things like that? I could fit extra door locks, check the window catches — even phone back and ask PC Wood if I could put in one of those alarms that ring straight through to the station. No doubt the damn things cost the earth, but never mind. How long did dealers persecute the kids they snared? Weeks? Months? Or would this added nightmare, like Malachy's miserable addiction, go on for years?

And then it struck — the thought that brought my calculations to a halt. Where was the rule that said that only one person in a marriage could disappear? Stuart had shown the way. He'd slid out of job and home without a trace. If I in turn wanted to rid myself of the miasma of trouble that clung to Malachy, what better way of doing it than vanishing myself?

CHAPTER
SEVEN

Within a week I had embarked on three new ventures. I'd been in touch with a solicitor to file for a divorce. I'd started looking for a brand-new job. And I'd arranged for the house to be put on the market.

I told the estate agent my husband worked abroad. ("But he's left all the paperwork I need to sign for the sale.") She didn't appear to think it strange that I wanted no signs outside the house, or advertisements in the papers. Indeed, she implied that slipping the word only to parties she thought might take a real interest in a property of this sort might work in my favour.

And so it seemed. Martin leaned over the fence a couple of times to tell me, "Jan says that woman with the red Renault let herself into your house again today, Lois. She had an elderly couple with her this time."

I had become as glib a liar as my son. "Showing her parents round, I expect. I take it Jan told you I'm renting out one of the bedrooms?"

"A good idea. I'm sure you could do with the company." (Ah, so the Tallentires had realized I was now alone.) From Martin's tone I grasped the hidden message: "That might keep you sane," and once again the certainty that talk of my frenzied attack on Tansy's boyfriend was running up and down the street set my stomach a-squirm. So I took little urging when, in an astonishingly short time, an offer for the house lay on the table. ("Go on," the estate agent said to me cheerfully. "You never know how long it will be till the next one. So take it. Move on.") The couple bought the curtains and the carpets, and threw in such a low offer for the dining table and chairs that they were astonished when I accepted that as well.

But I'd stopped worrying about money. Only the day before, I'd started a proper accounting job with a small family firm, Hanley & Hanley, run by a somewhat tottery but sharp old fellow and his engaging son. The hours were longer and the shared room drab, with lighting that made everyone look sallow. But I consoled myself with the good salary, telling myself that now that the house sale was agreed, I could look for a smaller place — a neat sunny flat with a balcony. If I chose well, I could get rid of most of my commitments and take my time to look for a more pleasant workplace.

A flat with a balcony, then! De-cluttering my life became a passion, and I was ruthless. In that last couple of weeks I took particular pleasure in smuggling boxes out of the house into the back of my car. Early one morning Jan slopped out in her dressing gown to stop her side gate banging in the breeze and called across, "They certainly must be keeping you busy at that new job of yours, Lois, if you're having to schlep this amount of stuff back and forth every day."

I simply smiled. I'd wait until the coast was clear to slip out some unwanted painting or a nest of stools to give to a charity shop or drop off for auction. I cleaned the house from top to bottom. I mowed the tiny lawn before I sold the mower. I even borrowed my own ladder back to wash the windows. Nor did I neglect the matter of paperwork. Like Stuart, I fixed up a box number for mail that might follow, but, unlike him, I took the time to write the details on a piece of card with a brief note for our son. "*Dear Malachy, I won't nag. But when you're done with all that poisonous stuff, this is how you can get back in touch. All my love, Mum.*"

It seemed so horribly inadequate. I tore it into pieces. This was my boy, after all. I'd nursed him, cuddled and bathed him, taught him how to tie his shoelaces — the million small intimacies between mother and child. How could the two of us have found ourselves beached up this way? Forgetting for a moment that he was the cause of all this upheaval, I thought of writing, "*Oh, Malachy, sweetie. Come away with me. I'll give you one last chance if you just promise to <u>try</u>.*" But what would have been the point? He'd have been heading back to his old haunts within a matter of hours. So in the end I wrote the first note out again, except for the word "stuff". "Stuff" was too weak a word for what had put an end to all my dreams of family. They called it "shit" and shit it was. So that's what I called it, and then, because that's such an ugly word, I didn't simply seal the envelope; I stuck on sticky tape just to be sure that no one else would read it by mistake.

I picked a lunch hour when I knew Soraya would be working on her own to drop the envelope off at SwiftClean. I tried to sound casual: "I think I've lost Malachy again. If he comes in to find me, would you give him this?"

Soraya took it with a worried look. "It isn't *cash*?"

Leaving a box number for your own son sounds so unloving that I lied. "No, it's my new mobile number."

She slid the envelope between the wall and the radio, where we had always kept the bits and pieces with no proper home. I hung round chatting till the next customer showed up, then slid away to pick up the keys to the small service flat I'd rented for a month.

That Saturday, at a time when I knew the Tallentires would be out shopping, the van I'd ordered came to clear out every last thing and take it to a lock-up. I scribbled one more note: "*As I told Martin, I decided to sell after all . . . family illness in South Africa . . . stuff in storage . . . send you a proper address . . . feel free to keep the ladder.*" I knew poor Martin would get a proper ticking-off. "She says she *told* you. Honestly!" And yet the note would satisfy their curiosity enough to stop them asking questions. They would have something to tell the other neighbours and, if I knew the world, all but my menacing telephone callers would soon forget me.

I dropped the envelope through the Tallentires' letter box and left a collection of my least favourite plants on their back step to add a touch of verisimilitude to my claim to be leaving the country. And then I scarpered. I said goodbye to no one. I said nothing at work. I simply slid into the delicious anonymity of 14F Forum Buildings, and used the long light summer evenings to look for somewhere permanent to live.

In the end I chose Pickstone, a not-frightfully-attractive dormer village eight miles the other side of the city. I dropped the idea of a flat and chose instead a little terraced house. It looked like nothing from the outside, but whoever had owned it had made the most of space and light and colour. The pocket-handkerchief garden was enchanting and the place so cheap that all my outlays would be more than covered by my new salary.

And that was furnished by a job I came to love. Even the biliously lit workplace became a pleasure. One morning Trevor Hanley and his father both came in beaming. "Right, ladies. We want all of you to work at home next week from Monday till Friday."

Audrey and Dana wheedled and probed. But the Hanleys were adamant. "No explanations." "You'll find out soon enough."

It was a soothing few days. I worked in the early mornings and the evenings and took the chance to use the rest of the time to shop for all those fiddly things you find you need after a move. Without the office chatter, I finished everything in half the time. On Thursday I even considered calling in for yet another batch of clients' files to tide me over. But in the end I spent the time in my garden. From the sheer stillness around me I could tell that soon the summer would be drawing to an end. I sat in the tiny arbour and wondered how I could be so happy after so many wasted years. It seemed to me that most other women who were in my position could tell themselves they'd salvaged something: "But then again I got two lovely daughters out of it", "Mind you, we had some good times", "I'd have to admit I saw a bit of the world." As for myself, sitting there in thickening dusk, I supposed that at least I had learned the value of absence. To have the two people in the world who had so thoroughly drained my crystals well and truly gone was, it seemed, pretty much all it took to make me happy. Had I been *born* wanting so little? Or had I learned the hard way that you can do without anything in life except for simple peace of mind?

On Monday I found Audrey and Dana waiting for me on the office steps. "They've locked us out."

Even as Audrey made the complaint, the door swung open and Trevor Hanley flung his arms wide to greet us. "Surprise!"

A giant picture window had appeared. It ran the length of the office. Those horrid lights had been switched off and daylight flooded in. I was astonished. I hadn't realized up till then that the ugly and featureless room in which we'd been working was directly above the canal path. Birches and willows. Reed-warblers. Even goldfinches. From that day on my workplace was a double joy, for I have always been content dealing with numbers. Numbers do as they're told. They are predictable. No half-tones in accounts. Add up the figures. You are either right or you are wrong. The columns balance or don't. It's the most satisfying and soothing of occupations. There are no trailing ends. You can be happy. And if each time you raise your head you see a swan float past, or moorhens dabbling on the far bank, or a young mother pushing a child in a stroller alongside the canal, then it is possible to feel all's right with the world.

For over a year I worked there, snug as toast. Audrey and Dana were pleasant company. Nobody pressed me for details about my life. (I had the feeling that, sensing I might have secrets behind me, they made a point of not prying.) From time to time young Mr Hanley or his father would ask a question about my plans for the weekend and, without telling lies, I'd manage to create the impression that I was busy with distant family. I wondered if the other two women had me down for something dramatic — perhaps a murderess out on licence, given the job through the good offices of both kindly Hanleys? But then once, when I put my hand on Dana's back as I squeezed past between two sets of filing cabinets and she moved sharply aside, I wondered if they'd formed the view that I might be a lesbian, and that was the reason why they never pressed me, as they did seem to be constantly pressing one another, on the matter of men, and children, and how I spent my time at the weekends.

But it is possible, of course, that their reserve sprang from the fact that they simply found me boring: a woman whose passage through the office could raise no ripples and could leave no wake. I wasn't bothered. It all suited me, and I felt so content that it even made me smile when, walking behind the cabinets one day well into the lunch hour, I heard a snatch of Trevor Hanley's conversation with his father.

"Of course I like her. Why would I have agreed to take her on if I didn't like her?"

There was a muffled reply from further in the room, and then a burst of laughter.

"Invite her out? Lois? Jesus Christ, Dad! The woman's far too cool a customer for someone like me!"

CHAPTER
EIGHT

Too cool a customer. Was I? Yes, probably. Back in the worst time, when Malachy was still in school and I was mad with anxiety about him and his future, Mrs Kuperschmidt suggested a course of family therapy. Stuart refused point blank. "The only problem in this family is that boy mixing with all those losers and druggies."

I couldn't budge him so I decided to go alone with Malachy. It took forever even to get an appointment, and that was for some weeks ahead. When I reminded Malachy, two days before, he irritably claimed he couldn't make it — off to a gig in Sheffield with some mates.

"But it's a school day."

He gave me one of those "you sad, sad woman" looks I spent my whole life trying to ignore. I fought back. "I'm really sorry, Malachy. But you're just going to have to tell your friends that you're not going. This has been fixed for weeks."

He didn't show up, of course. So I went in by myself — mostly, I told myself, to try to explain how an appointment I'd fussed so much to get had ended up being treated so lightly. But in my heart I knew I'd come for solace. The therapist looked the sort — restful and elegant in the strangely shaped chair she told me was "ergonomically designed" and which allowed her to lean forward in apparent ease while I was telling her the sorry tale of how things with my son had gone so painfully wrong. In the whole forty minutes I was sitting there, she can have interrupted only once or twice to steer me up some fresh path, or, to my astonishment, ask me a question that gave me reason to believe she'd even put aside the time to read the file.

And then, to my surprise, instead of spooning out advice on stubborn husbands or on wayward sons, she'd told me that each time I found myself surrounded by worries I was to stop in my tracks and tell them that I was busy, but that I'd make an appointment for them to come back at another time.

I simply thought that I'd misunderstood. "Excuse me? Make an appointment with my *worries*?"

"That's right."

"You mean, as if they're *people*?"

"Yes."

While I was staring at her — was she *mad*? — she added sternly, "Of course, it's very important that you keep the appointments you make. If things get busy, you can reschedule, of course. But you must never fob your worries off. They just won't stand for it."

I couldn't get out fast enough. I even thought of phoning Mrs Kuperschmidt to tell her the woman she'd been so keen to recommend was little more than a down-and-out charlatan. But that night, as I lay worrying that Malachy wasn't home, resentful that

Stuart was uncaringly asleep as usual, fretting about everything, I'd given it a go. Because the whole business sounded such a farce, I took it lightly, even making a little private joke of it. "I'm sorry, worries," I drawled to them silently inside my head in what I took to be a Californian accent. "I simply can't be dealing with you now. I have a busy day tomorrow and need my sleep. So you all mosey along and come back tomorrow at —"

I paused to consider. Stuart brought up the tea at seven, then promptly vanished downstairs to the computer.

"— at five past seven. I'll worry with you then."

I pulled up the covers, rolled over and fell fast asleep.

Next thing I knew, Stuart was chinking his way back through the door into the bedroom, carrying the tray. "*You* had a good night."

"I did, didn't I?" The first of my worries rushed back. "Is Malachy home?"

"Flat out in bed. The kitchen *reeks* of cigarette smoke."

Feeling like someone in a fairy tale granted a precious wish, I kept my part of the bargain. As soon as Stuart had hurried off, I leaned back on the pillows. "All right, worries. I'm all yours. What shall we fret about?"

They hadn't much to say. Only the same old stuff. Even if I managed to rouse him, would Malachy bother to show up at school? Would he need a cover note for bunking off, and, if he did, should I provide it or provoke yet another horrible scene by telling him I wouldn't? Was he truly asleep, or lying there dead from an overdose? Would he, some day, set fire to the house with all these late-night cigarettes? When had I last gone round and checked the smoke alarms?

That sort of thing. I tried to worry about each in turn. Then, since there seemed so little to be added (and, in my mind, my little worries half admitted it, even among themselves), I simply rose a few minutes earlier than usual, tested all three alarms, and drove off, rested, to work. Halfway along Hawtrey Road it suddenly occurred to me that sooner or later Malachy might start bringing "friends" home from all these rock concerts of his — friends who lived way out of town, or who'd been locked out by sterner, tougher parents. Even, perhaps, ne'er-do-wells he'd only that evening met in some pub and —

Pulling myself together, I saw my worries off with cast-iron confidence. "Sorry," I told them. "Right now I'm busy driving, and then I'll be at work. How about nine o'clock tonight when I'm in my bath. That any good for you?"

Over the years I'd blessed that therapist in my head over and over. I even managed to refine the skill she taught me till it worked for almost anything. Show me another woman who could have had a marriage for so many years, then have it end, kept track of all the paperwork through two full house moves, seen off the only two men who tried to date her (one in the hardware store and one who replaced the tyres on my car) and put her divorce papers safely away in a fireproof box without a single tear. You can fight disappointments or, like me, you can let them take your heart and shrivel it as surely as a tribe of cannibals will shrink a head. I'd let it happen and I had been grateful. I'd used that little trick the therapist had taught me, and then abused it, till I had learned the art of brushing aside anything that should have bothered me.

So Trevor Hanley was right. I was too cool a customer for any man to fancy. Not that it bothered me. I liked to know that I was so impregnable that nothing could touch me. I even watched my own birthday come and go, unremarked by anyone, without a flicker — apart from the reminder that later that month it would be Malachy's too. Halfheartedly I did begin to gather a few goodies in a cardboard carton: a book of cartoons, tea bags and chocolate, the tins of lychees he had always loved. But then I broke into the package of tea bags and after that, instead of pressing on to fill the box, I simply emptied it out. I wasn't in the mood to go and trawl the city streets for my son, knowing from long experience that there was nothing I could do to change his current way of life. If he was desperate, or ill, or worryingly thin, I didn't want to know.

I didn't want to *care*. I was too busy, loving my little house, loving my plants, loving my pretty garden arbour. I went for great long walks. I took a painting class. I cooked more, taught myself to sew and spent hours listening to the radio. I liked the daily drive into the city. I liked the way that both the Hanleys took a few minutes from their own work each day to stroll behind our desks, cooing our praises. When Audrey and

Dana eyed one another as the clock came round to half past five, and closed their box files, I took great satisfaction in stacking things for the morning, then sliding my chair in neatly under my desk just as we had at school. I'd say goodbye to Dana on the steps, then walk with Audrey as far as her Queen's Park bus stop before taking off down yet another street, towards the car park.

And it was there one light spring evening that, pulling out of the exit, I braked to let a pregnant woman cross the road in front of me. I hadn't even made her break her stride, but she was clearly the sort hair-triggered to take offence. Even before she stepped off the kerb she was giving me the finger. Strutting in front of my car, she made the effort to swing her arm around so she could keep up the offensive gesture. And though my window was rolled up I could still hear her piercing yell. "You stupid trout! Get off the fucking pavement! Bitch!"

It was the voice from under the canal bridge. I stared at her, appalled. Could that be Malachy's baby she was carrying? Oh, dear gods, no! Surely from one glance you could see she was the sort of young woman who'd get through boys and men as fast as other people get through underwear.

My look of horror set off a fresh wave of abuse. "What are you staring at, you prissy bitch? You had your eyeful? Stupid, stupid cow!"

Panicking, I glanced in my rear mirror. Just for once, no one was behind me. I slammed the car into reverse and shot back, giving myself just enough space to swing around and drive instead past the NO EXIT sign.

And once again I was lucky. No one was driving in. Without a thought for any penalties if I were caught, I shot out of the entrance and off down the street. As soon as I dared, I took a look behind me. The witchy creature was still standing blocking the exit, probably still shrieking after me as, trembling so hard that I could barely keep a grip on the wheel, I reached the roundabout at the end of the street and took the very first turning — not the road I wanted at all — simply because it was clear.

CHAPTER
NINE

Safe home, I took stock. How had the sight of this young woman so managed to rattle me? She didn't know who I was. And who was to say that it was Malachy's baby? How long ago had I heard them quarrelling under the bridge, and followed them along the canal path? A whole lot longer than nine months. There was no reason to think that someone as feckless as Malachy would stick at such a troubled relationship, and she didn't look the sort to keep her knees together very long.

But still I couldn't put the worry out of mind. Something went wrong. The simple trick I'd used through all my previous upheavals had deserted me. I fretted till my brain bled. From what I'd seen, the birth could easily be imminent. Over the past year I'd managed not to go out and scour the city for my son, yet now when I read the local evening paper, my eye fell first on snippets about babies that had been born in taxis or supermarket aisles; and though there was nothing about the girl I'd seen that would lead anyone to think she was the sort to want to see the words "Proud father Malachy" set into print, I took to studying the birth announcements. Over and again I'd try to get a grip, reminding myself how very unlikely it was that her baby could be any grandchild of mine. And yet I couldn't help but be aware that, on the excuse of only two days of roadworks, I seemed to have changed my route to and from work. Now I drove down the long, long street on which I'd watched the two of them catching the bus all that time ago, and more than once over the next couple of months, instead of turning off on to the road to Pickstone, I kept on north, tracking the route of 18A request stops as far as Forth Hill and Danbury, keeping my eyes peeled through those grim estates.

Each time, I asked myself why. After all, no one is mad enough to go out searching for a daughter-in-law with a vile attitude and a foul temper. But I had built a fantasy on one small fact: she'd not been smoking. Perhaps, though it made her so irritable she'd pick a fight with a stranger, she'd managed to give up the habit for the sake of the baby. Maybe Malachy had too. And if he could give up one addictive thing, why not another? Bad habits reinforce one another. Maybe the shock of finding out they would be parents had forced the two of them to clean up their druggie act. It wasn't likely. But it was possible. Anything was *possible*.

And then it would be up to me to mend our fences. I knew exactly what was lost when a rift settles in a family. The last thing on earth I wanted to do to my son was treat him the way I'd been treated. I couldn't bear to think that he might simmer with resentments even a fraction as strong as those I'd ended up holding against my mother and father. I would go mad even to think it.

He knew why he'd been asked to leave the house. He'd sat there sulking as Mrs Kuperschmidt had done the business of explaining exactly why it was impossible for him to stay. He hadn't argued. He had understood. But it had been my decision to let him slide entirely out of touch. So now it was my job to find out more. If Malachy was off drugs then, even if his new child's mother wasn't the partner I would choose for him — and she most definitely was not — then I would bite the bullet.

But there were other voices in my head — sensible voices that had no truck with fantasy, and took a different tack. They crowded in, reminding me how grim life with Malachy had been, assuring me that young men like him don't throw off addiction that easily. After the efforts I'd had to make to spirit myself safely away, it would be madness to risk being spotted. My son might see me driving past and follow to find out where I lived.

I wasn't the only person who could do the job, though. If whole hosts of suspicious wives could get their husbands followed, then surely I could find someone to track my son down, take a look, and report back.

No sooner had I had the thought than caution intervened. I'd taken so much trouble to cover my traces. Now I'd be inviting some unknown professional to bridge the precious gap between my old life and my new. Did I really want to put myself at the mercy of somebody else's skills and discretion? I didn't mind the tax office knowing where I'd gone. The gas and phone companies sent bills, and that too was fine by me. That was computers. But take the risk of asking a living person to track down my son to see if he and Trouble were still firm friends? That was a different story.

On my brain gurned. Disguise, then. How about a floppy hat? Or headscarf?

Both dismissed at once. I'd spent too many hours at SwiftClean not to have realized how mistaken any woman is to think that what she wears can make that sort of difference. You may hear "You look ten years younger," — even "It makes you look a very different kind of person." But "I'd not have recognized you in a million years"? Oh, no. You don't hear that.

A wig, then. I could disguise myself by buying a wig! I thumbed through the Yellow Pages and was quite shocked to see how many wig-makers could make a living in just one city. It sent my thinking up a strange old path. Before she died, had my own mother's hair come out in handfuls? Could she have so despaired of the pink patches spreading hotch-potch on her skull that even she had gathered up the courage to walk through the doors of one of these places that so discreetly advertised their skills? I suddenly remembered her only headscraf, a swirly orange and yellow affair she'd rarely worn but I had loved, and rippled round my head through all my childhood "ballet shows" and "fairy dances". Had she worn that as she inched shyly through the door to get advice? I couldn't bear to think I might go somewhere she had been in such sad straits. I chose a place my mother would have found far too intimidating, on one of those hidden little back streets where pricey and sophisticated dress shops with bells on the door deter all but the most confident shoppers. My mother would have made excuses and fled if she'd been greeted with the same urbanity with which the "salon" owner greeted me. Her calm soft-spoken patter drew out the chosen lie: "One or two friends suggested I'd face the treatments with more confidence if I know, even if my hair falls out, I'll have the option . . ."

She sat me at a mirror inside an elegant little cubicle hung on three sides with grey drapes. In all the things she tugged down on my head I looked exactly like myself, but better.

"You see, I was thinking of a change."

"If it's to cover temporary hair loss —"

I tried to look the "fun" sort. "But it seems such a waste to choose something that looks so like my own. I thought it would be good to have something different. If I do have to wear it, it will make a change. And if I don't, then I can use it after."

"After?"

"To wear to parties," I explained.

"*Parties?*"

"You know," I faltered. "Fancy dress. Charades and stuff. That sort of thing."

She was appalled. Thinking I must still be in shock from hearing my diagnosis, she murmured to her assistant to bring back the cup of coffee I'd hesitated over for just a moment before refusing. While we were waiting, she worriedly fixed her eyes on my reflection and tried to persuade me into yet another soft brown affair that mirrored my own hair but made me look younger.

I pulled it off. "I'd like to be a redhead."

"It's always best, we find, to —"

But I had swivelled round to point at a wig on the display shelf behind us. "That one there."

"I really do think you should consider —"

"Yes. That one. Definitely that one."

She wasn't happy, frowning in a most unprofessional way as she adjusted it on my head. Her whole demeanour made it obvious she thought my walking round in it would be the worst possible advertisement for her shop. I got the feeling she only let me have it because she feared I might be able to bring some action against her if she refused for no good reason that anyone (except those with judgement) could see. Certainly no one can ever have made it quite so unspokenly clear to a stranger how much they hope that their imminent medical treatment will not result in hair loss.

But she did take my measurements and fill in the form. Two weeks, she warned, but maybe the order haunted her so badly she pushed it to the top of the list because the package arrived only a few days later. The small brown box was so discreet that finding the wig inside it took me by surprise. I pulled it on and looked at myself all ways in the mirror.

Appalling. Almost a fright wig. Forget about fancy-dress parties. This was fit only for Hallowe'en. I cursed myself for wasting half a month's salary on some bubbling red monstrosity I'd never dare to wear. And then, in some despair and irritation, I fetched the scissors.

Once it was shorter it did at least look less like a joke. I tipped my head this way and that, making the curls bounce and practising casually chatting to my new self in the mirror. I cut off a little bit more. Now it looked even better, and I could almost imagine passing through crowds of distracted shoppers without everyone staring. What if I just —?

The doorbell rang.

Pulling the wig off, I ran a comb through my own flattened hair and hurried to the door.

Two police officers stood waiting, one man, one woman. "Mrs Henderson?"

From the way that the woman was wringing her cap in her hands, I knew already and tried to slam the door shut. "No!"

This way of trying to see off bad news can't be unusual. The other officer was already using his foot to jam the door open. "Mrs Henderson, please let us in."

"No! Go away! Go!"

But why I said it with such vehemence I'll never know, because already I had given up the fight. An arm was laid around my shoulder and I was ushered back into my own living room. "Mrs Henderson. Come and sit down. *Please.*"

They hovered till I was safely on the sofa, then sat down, both uncomfortably leaning as if poised to catch me. It never occurred to me that they had come about Stuart. Why should it? My vanished husband had picked his way far, far too carefully through life to suffer accidents.

"It's Malachy?"

Yes, it was Malachy. And yes, my son was dead. Not from an overdose, it seemed, but from a scuffle because of a stupid drug debt. One kick too many had sent him sliding down the bank into the canal. And for some reason that would be left to the coroner to rule on, he wasn't in a good enough state to scramble out. My hand was being patted. I watched the dust motes in a shaft of light and waited for the gentle burblings of two well-meaning people to draw to an end. "These thugs don't bat an eyelid. Owe them too much and they turn into animals. They don't care if you leave a young mother and a twelve-week-old son."

I turned to stare. A boy, then.

Three months old.

The woman officer was still rabbiting on. I couldn't stop her. "There'll be a full criminal investigation, of course. But, in the circumstances . . ." From the shrug it was clear that even someone defending themselves against a lesser charge than murder could probably put up quite a passable defence. Rather reluctantly, she finished up, "It seems your son was very drunk."

Instantly her companion changed tack. "You really shouldn't sit here by yourself. Can we phone someone for you?"

Of course, there was no one. And that's what set me thinking. "How did you know where to find me?"

His face took on a look of deep unease. The woman, meanwhile, picked her words with obvious care. "Of course, our only *official* responsibility is to the next of kin."

What was she saying? Surely if anyone was Malachy's next of kin, then it was —

Ah!

Can shock be real and still shot through with cunning? "Malachy's wife?"

"Yes. Janie Gay."

A name for her at last, then. Janie Gay. And they were married! And all I could feel was utter contempt for that part of myself that recognized my son was dead yet still took the chance to murmur with utter mildness, "Yes, of course," to make them think I'd known that all along.

"But Mrs Kuperschmidt was in the station picking up somebody's file when —" She stopped. I knew she must be glazing over something horrible she thought I didn't need to know. "Anyhow, the desk officer was on the phone about arrangements. She overheard him saying Malachy's name and told him she'd dealt with your family over a number of years and wasn't sure —"

Another stutter to a halt.

"In short, she wasn't sure quite how you'd come to hear the news and didn't want you to stumble on it in tomorrow's papers. We did ask Janie Gay for your address, but I'm afraid —" There was another long, long pause. "Well, she wasn't in a fit state to help with your details. But Mrs Kuperschmidt did say that since you and Malachy had never formally put a stop to the counselling, we would be justified in —"

Ah! So their worries were about *procedures*. Kind Mrs Kuperschmidt had pushed them into twisting rules. My head was bleached of sense. How could I even be making space for thoughts like these when there was Malachy — no, when there *wasn't* Malachy — when —

The officer was still explaining. "And there are channels we can use to find a person's address when it's — *important*."

I didn't have to play her hesitation through again to know that she'd pulled back from saying "when it's a death". And once again I was distracted by the sheer astonishment of finding I could lose my son and still have room in my brain to wonder at the graciousness and tact of someone else's daughter.

And then I forced myself up, up, and up some more, till I was standing. I took their hands. I thanked them and assured them both that I'd be fine. I promised I would phone if I could think of anything that anyone could do. I took the leaflet that they offered me called *Help at Hand* and laid it carefully aside, for all the world as if I were going to keep it, not simply rip it into pieces and stuff it in the bin. I showed them to the door and gave a little wave as they walked down my path, still thanking them sincerely for bringing me the news of Malachy lying on a marble slab — kicked, beaten, drowned, and lost to me for ever.

CHAPTER
TEN

The other kind words came from Mrs Kuperschmidt. Just as I stepped into the bath on one of those first black, everlasting evenings that followed the dreadful visit, another police car drew up outside and before I could put on my dressing gown and hurry down, something had dropped through the letter box.

It was a note: "*I was so very sorry to hear . . .*"

I wondered why she hadn't posted it, then realized the officers' unofficial favour had not extended to passing on my address. She said she could offer no comfort except to say that in her experience grief had a life of its own. It was born — kicking strong and greedy, and draining everyone around of every ounce of energy. Then, as time passed, it grew more settled: one could live with it. And in the end, just like a person, it would age and die, to leave only memories. She wrote her phone number at the top, and then again in the last paragraph. She said she hoped to see me on Tuesday morning at the crematorium, but she was finding it difficult to sort out an adequate replacement for some important duty that had been booked for weeks.

I studied her letter like runes, knowing she'd guessed why I had slid away from my old neighbourhood, blessing her for her tact, and for the clue she was giving me to the time and place of my son's funeral.

His funeral . . . The very word came as a shock. All those long nights I'd pictured Malachy's battered frame gathering enough speed down the slope to roll across the gritty path, into the filthy canal. I'd heard his outraged howls and watched his desperate thrashings as he tried over and over to find a handhold on the steep brick side. I'd watched in agony as his befuddled brain finally stopped making the effort. I saw him dragged out in a tangle of weeds, slimy with mud. Burying my head beneath the covers, I tried to blot out my imaginings: the catcalls of his tormentors; the sheer indifference of exhausted paramedics to a young body well past help or feeling; even the scream of post-mortem tools at their grim business. All of these horrifying visions seared my brain over and over. And yet it wasn't till Mrs Kuperschmidt's note arrived that it came home to me that, all this time, phones had been ringing, men and women in sober suits had been making appointments and offering catalogues and price options — perhaps even a loan repayment schedule. All was discussed and agreed.

My son was going to have a funeral.

I rang the crematorium. Yes, Tuesday, they confirmed. At nine o'clock. I put the phone down, blushing. Nine in the morning? Surely that had to be the least favoured time — even the cheapest? I thought of telling my father. He was the only family I had left. Twice I snatched up my bag and hurried to the car. The first time I didn't even get as far as switching on the engine. The next, I made it all the way to the end of our old street, then turned and drove straight back because I'd suddenly realized that he'd be expecting me. He would be sitting waiting, just as he'd waited so patiently through my mother's last desperate illness. He'd know about Malachy's death. He might not read the papers every day, but one of his neighbours was bound to have spotted that little square of print, giving the name and the age of the body pulled out of the water. I'd cut around it carefully and slid it in a drawer. My father would have done the same. Oh, he'd be waiting, busily honing condolences to use as a battering ram. "So, Lois. You *have* been unlucky with your family." I could already see him standing accusingly, shaking his head in the way that would send his real message: "Look at you, Lois! You've killed your mother, driven off your husband, quarrelled with me, and been such a poor parent your son never even reached twenty!"

He didn't need me to tell him the time and place of any funeral. I knew him only too well. He would have phoned round every church and crematorium in the book till he hit lucky. And he'd be there at the back. He'd introduce himself to no one. I'd probably be the only person there who knew who he was, but he wouldn't nod my way. He'd simply stand there in his best suit, staring ahead and making himself impregnable by putting himself in the right. "No one can say I didn't go to my own grandson's funeral."

I wouldn't be able to *bear* it. I could imagine myself hurrying away at the mere sight of him. And what sort of mother did that make me? One worried more about avoiding a sneer from her father than burying her son. Across my misery ran a wash of shame, tinged with self-pity. For surely anyone else would have found herself free to mourn without the interference of ever-rising resentment against some member of the family not seen for years.

Which brought another problem straight to mind. What about Stuart? I had assumed he'd vanished from Malachy's life as swiftly and cleanly as he'd gone from mine. But who was to say the two of them hadn't been in touch again over the last couple of years? Wherever it was that Stuart was living now, he might have come back, even for a single day. Perhaps, like me, he'd spotted Malachy hanging around in some doorway or waiting for a bus. He could have stopped to speak. And if the months of distance had worked some magic, the two of them might have even strolled off together to share an amiable pint. A thousand possibilities ran through my mind and, hating my own father as I did for his stern, calculated cruelty in not telling me about my mother's death, I couldn't bear to think that someone else might one day claim I'd treated them in the same monstrous fashion. I'd live in terror, knowing that one day my bell might ring and Stuart would be on the doorstep. "For God's sake, Lois! Malachy was my son too! How could you not have tried to let me know?"

I thought things through till I was dizzy. I *wouldn't* look for Stuart. I would rather *die*. The craven coward he'd turned out to be must pay the price for sloping off without a word. I didn't *care*. Then, in an instant, all my fine reasons for doing nothing would be swept away in waves of shamed embarrassment as I imagined my former husband standing on my doorstep, listening to me try to defend them. After all, the police had tracked me down. Who was to say they couldn't find Stuart just as easily? A visit to his old workplace or a few phone calls to other government departments was all it would take. How could I kid myself there weren't a dozen ways in which, if the situation were reversed, I would feel justified in thinking that Stuart ought to have looked for me?

The weekend passed in a fog of guilt, then misery, then guilt again. I listened to the clock tell cold grey time. By Monday morning I knew I should be ringing Mr Hanley to tell him that I wouldn't be coming in — no, not today and not tomorrow either. And probably not the day after that. I'd pick up the phone and stand there, paralysed, until the welcoming silence turned to a warning buzz. I couldn't make the call. Oh, I could face his kindness, but not his astonishment. "Lois? Oh, Lois, I'm *mortified*. I didn't even realize you *had* a son. Oh, Lois, we're all so *sorry*." Before he'd even put down the phone there'd be a puzzled look on Audrey's face. "Lois? A *son*?" She'd turn to Dana for the confirmation that would appal them all: "I'm as surprised as you two. All of this time! And yet she never even mentioned him. What a strange thing!"

The sympathy of decent people so profoundly shocked would be intolerable. And so on Monday morning I got out of bed, put on my plain grey skirt and ruffled blouse and went to the office as usual. The

69

sun shone gloriously through the wide, freshly washed window. There was a heron standing in the reeds. I tried the old, old trick to put off anguish. "Wait until after work," I begged my sorrows and strains. "You've had the whole weekend. You'll have the whole of tomorrow. Please let me off for just an hour or two so I can rest in work." Desperate for the unfeeling clarity of numbers, I stared at shimmering columns. Nothing made sense. I checked things over and over and, even when sure I was right, still had to go back to check that the calculation I'd done was the one that was needed.

A shadow fell across my desk. "Lois?" Trevor Hanley was staring. "Lois, you're crying."

He laid a finger on my paperwork, then held it out for me to inspect. "That's a tear, Lois." It wasn't a question. And yet, as though to offer me the benefit of the doubt, he licked the tip of his finger.

It was a gesture of such intimacy that I was shocked. I sat in silence as he spread his huge hand to swivel my worksheet to face him. "Not like you, Lois."

Had he spotted a mistake? He swung a plump trousered leg across the corner of my desk. It was as if some schoolteacher had suddenly decided to park himself more comfortably while he ran through the principles of long division one more time with some dim pupil. "Lois, what's up? The ladies are telling me you're in an awful state. Your figures are all over. And you've been crying."

I hadn't made that massive effort to get up and come in, just to throw things away. "It's nothing, Trevor."

"It must be something."

"No, *honestly*." (The very word set off the urge to lie.) "It's only that I'm terrified of dentists, and I've an appointment for tomorrow morning." Catching his startled look, I added pathetically, "The only reason I haven't told you yet is because I'm still thinking of skipping it."

His face cleared. "Skip the dentist because you're scared? Oh, Lois, that won't do." Turning to Audrey and Dana, he offered them the excuse to admit that they'd been listening. "Which of you two is going to take poor Lois out for a drink after work? Give her some Dutch courage?"

Thank God, neither admitted to being free. Promptly at half past five I closed down my computer and crept away, crippled by shame. It seemed to me my stupid lie had robbed poor Malachy of his last shreds of dignity. Linking his funeral to something as trivial as a trip to the dentist, even in words alone as an excuse for absence, was nothing short of despicable. An insult to my son. But then again, right from the moment the officers had arrived on my doorstep with the bad news on their faces, everything I'd done and thought and felt had been unswervingly contemptible. I had to face the fact that over the last few days, when any decent woman would have spent her hours grieving properly, I'd spent mine being angry with my own father, and trying to conjure out of nowhere a sheer impossibility: a cast-iron explanation for not even trying to let another father know the date and time of his son's funeral.

Brains can't be tamed, though. And early in the morning, as I was pulling everything out of my closet

— black shoes, black bag, black dress, black coat — the lid fell off that small discreet brown box I'd thrown in sheer exasperation to the back.

Out of it fell not just the bright-red wig, but the solution.

Simple. Foolproof.

"I'm sorry, Stuart. But I didn't know about the funeral either. Ask anyone who went, and they will tell you that I wasn't there."

CHAPTER
ELEVEN

The wig-maker had done a better job for me than she would ever have thought. I wore a pair of rimmed glasses, kept my head down to let the partially tamed red curls cover my face, and waited until the last minute before getting out of my car and hurrying across to the chapel.

I can't think what I must have been expecting. A pack of drug-dealers with vulpine smiles? A host of tarts, all tottering on high heels and showing a deal too much skin? Maybe an empty chapel, with no one sitting there except my father.

A respectable number of people were spread across the pews, all looking comfortingly normal. I recognized one or two of Malachy's old mates from school: a lad with hair the colour of marmalade that flopped around so much it looked more like a wig than my own; another boy I'd always thoroughly disliked but who, in his sharp grey trousers and bright white shirt, might even have been able to convince me that in the years since I'd last seen him he had turned over a new leaf. There was a pew crammed altogether too tightly with girls. Almost without exception their hair was more garish than mine, and the whispers of one or two of them kept inappropriately approaching giggles. There was a man in a black suit who stood so straight I guessed he must be representing the police, and I was quite touched to think they took the time and showed the sensitivity to go to the funerals of people whose bodies they'd pulled from the water. Next to him stood a couple in dark but casual clothing. Were they plain-clothes officers? Or from the probation services? And was the fact that these three knew each other well enough to sit together proof that my Malachy's life had carried on with its slow slide?

And, sitting directly across the aisle from the three of them, there was my father. He'd turned at the creak of the door but looked my way with not a sign of recognition. A shiver of pure hatred ran down my spine. Just how cold was his heart? He must at least have *thought* I would be there for Malachy. Would it have killed him to have been waiting outside until the music soared, hoping to greet his only daughter, comfort her, and lead her in on his arm?

I took a seat at the back. I was the last in, but whole minutes passed. The whispering increased. Finally the canned organ dirge broke off and something much the same but a little more rousing started up instead. Everyone took it as a hint to stand, and, sure enough, almost at once in came the coffin with Janie Gay behind it. As she walked past, her high heels vulnerably wobbling as she was forced to slow her steps to match the coffin-bearers' steady pace, I sneaked a glance. She looked a whole lot better than I remembered. Both times I'd seen her before, of course, her face had been disfigured by snarls, and she had somehow managed to seem, at the same time, both bloated and half-starved. Now she looked much, much younger — almost Malachy's age — and, in her plain dark suit, a good deal less tarty. I found that a great comfort. Nobody likes to think their son was such a loser that he could end up sharing the last of his run-down life with some rock-bottom slattern who can't even scrub up for his funeral. Still, it was hard for me to melt with sympathy as she came past. I'd seen her martyred little look, as if my son's death had been one more irritation to make life awkward in a tiresome week.

It was a dismal service, straight from the printed pamphlet lying on the pew ledge, with no additions or readings, nor even any singing. Someone I took to be a crematorium employee did give a short address, saying exactly the sort of thing you would expect him to say about a young man he openly admitted he'd never met (and probably guessed hadn't amounted to much): "Everyone equally valuable in the sight of God . . . so much more sad when someone is cut down before their full potential can be realized" — that sort of thing. I tried as hard as I could to push away unruly thoughts crowding my brain. How was I going to get out at the end without speaking to anyone? Where was this famous baby? At one point I even found myself having to force down a rush of terror as I imagined my father churning in his mind something about the stance of that red-headed woman whom he'd watched walk in, then swinging round to point a finger. Even as the curtains were closing around the coffin I couldn't keep my Malachy in mind. Almost before the perfunctory service was over I'd sunk to my knees, prudently burying my face in my hands, as though in earnest prayer.

It wasn't long before the murmuring began, followed by the shuffling of feet and the rustle of abandoned pew sheets. I kept my face well hidden as all the other mourners made their way past, waiting till I was sure the chapel was empty before I warily raised my head and hurried to the back, past the collection plate that had stayed so dispiritingly empty.

I pushed the door open a crack. The lad with the floppy marmalade-coloured hair was down on one knee, struggling with a snapped lace as he continued to discuss with a friend the people who'd been present. "Her? She was a drug nark, I thought. Dressed like one, anyway. And that one sitting right in front of you was one of Janie Gay's cast-offs, back for some more." Scrambling to his feet, he inspected his watch. "Stopping off for a drink?"

"At Janie Gay's? Why not?"

"Know the way?"

"I'll follow you."

"I'm on the bike over there."

"Don't lose me in that warren. I'll never find my way out."

And they were off, crunching in different directions across the gravel. I felt a surge of relief that I'd escaped without being recognized and in an instant it had turned to rage that, even now, leaving my own son's funeral, my father was still uppermost in my mind. I forced myself to think of Malachy. What had his life been like over the last couple of years? By the time he died, had he and this peculiarly changeable Janie Gay — domineering girlfriend, vituperative citizen, vulnerable widow — managed to build a shared life — been happy, even? Maybe out there in Forth Hill — or, God forbid, Danbury — they'd managed to put together a halfway decent home, ready for their new baby. What was it like? Somewhere in one of those endless interlocking streets rife with infuriating cul-de-sacs to thwart the novice visitor, had Malachy been able to step out of his own little house into a garden? Or had the two of them ended up in one of those grim tower blocks the council had thrown up around the edges, where tenants had to stumble down flight after flight of stinking communal stairs to emerge in some litter-strewn yard? When Malachy looked out each morning, what had he seen? The shadow of some other ugly building looming over him, or a green waving tree? And had the sun reached down enough for him to hang in the window the only thing he'd ever bothered to take away with him from our old home: that tiny multi-faceted glass ball he'd loved so much through childhood, which caught the light and tossed its rainbow dots all round the room — bright splatterings of colour that in the last few years we were together it had exasperated me so much to watch him set dancing with a touch, over and over.

I'd never know.

Unless —

Not even offering myself the chance to change my mind, I stepped back into the chapel. Already an usher was passing between the pews, skilfully gathering up the battered old pamphlets from Malachy's bog-standard service with one hand while slapping down specially printed sheets for the next with the other.

I tugged off the wig and ran my fingers through my hair, trying to unflatten it. I almost ran to my car. Parking it close to the gates had given me so much of a head start that by the time the huge black motorbike roared past, I was already in gear. In other circumstances they might have noticed that the same small blue car was right behind them all the way. But I suppose a part of their attention was on the leading and the following. In any case, what were they going to think? Some woman driving in the same direction. What's special about that? I didn't even take the risk of keeping back too far, or trying not to turn a corner till they were round the next. Each time I spotted a street sign I muttered the name of it under my breath until I saw the next. I never really thought I'd get to follow them the whole way to the house. But, almost without warning, the car ahead of me slewed to the kerb behind the motorbike while I sailed past, glancing from left to right in a desperate hunt for some house name or number.

One hundred and forty-two, or thereabouts. And still in Forth Hill, thank God. We hadn't gone as far as Danbury. I slowed the car to a crawl until I'd spotted in the rear-view mirror which gate they pushed. Then I drove on, checking the street name once again at the next corner, then pulling to the side myself to scribble what I thought was the address down on a petrol receipt.

And then I sat and thought. Dare I go back and drive past slowly again?

No. I had shot my only bolt of courage. I'd come back later, in my own good time. Even walk past. But now I felt done in. All the way home, I felt uneasy. For God's sake, Lois, I kept on telling myself. You've just this minute stood to watch your own son's body slide into an oven to be burned to ashes. Give yourself a break.

I drove home carefully, as if through flames.

CHAPTER
TWELVE

Grief's strange. The Malachy in my head was two, or six, or a rambunctious twelve — anything other than the age he'd been when his life ended. How old was he when I last saw him? I worked it out to the exact day and hour and was astonished to realize it was a calculation I'd never have to make again. How *long* it was since I saw him — that would change every day. It might even, if I lived long enough, rise into tens of years. But just how old he was the day I watched him swallowed up by that green bus — well, that would never change, not by a single minute.

The nights were long. I don't remember crying. But then again, I rarely have, except in childhood when I trapped my fingers in a doorway or fell out of a tree. Classmates who cried at school always repelled me. I'd turn away rather than see those spurting teardrops and open wet mouths. I hated the howling, and couldn't understand how teachers could stand so close, or help to mop those slimy reddened faces.

No, what I remember of the next few months is the dull thud that echoed in my chest like a twin heartbeat. Sometimes I could forget that it was there. Sometimes I couldn't. One night I came home with a bottle of gin.

I'm not a drinker. I don't know how to do it, or when to stop. That first time, I poured out the tiniest amount, drowned it in lemonade and never even bothered to finish it. The next night, I drank a whole big tumbler, almost neat, and then threw up. In my disgust, I thought of emptying the bottle down the sink; but in the end my thrifty instincts made me shove it out of sight behind the cornflakes. I spent a lot of time on the canal path underneath the arch where I'd first come across this Janie Gay, wondering whether, if I'd called down to my son instead of simply following the two of them along to that bus stop, I might have somehow altered the course of things. After a death there's no other way to look than backwards. Was it too much I did on that occasion? Or too little there? I must have done *something* wrong to cause the end of things in such a way.

Then I'd remind myself that that is what it was. The end. Week after week I scoured the crematorium grounds for some new urn or recently set plaque bearing my son's name. But nothing, always nothing. One morning, after yet another hour's fruitless search, I walked between the mock Palladian pillars into their reception office. "I was just wondering —"

"Yes?"

"How you find out where someone . . . Where . . ."

The grey-haired woman jumped with practised ease into my hesitation. "Where someone's ashes have been interred?" Her voice was tender. "You couldn't possibly give me a name?"

The question was so ludicrous I felt like snapping. In all her experience of working behind that desk, had anyone *ever* come in to ask for help in finding the last remains of someone whose name they hadn't known? Instead I said with what I hoped was a suitable level of reverence, "It's Henderson. Malachy Henderson."

It only took a moment for her to — as she so unfortunately termed it — "bring him up". Lifting her eyes from the screen, she told me, equally softly, "I'm awfully sorry but, as yet, there's nowhere I can direct you for that name."

I wanted to bellow at her, "He is not a *name*. He was my *son*." But the bereaved must quickly learn to act with perfect meekness. Release a fraction of your murderous feelings, and every human contact would vanish at once.

Timidly I echoed, "Nowhere to direct me?"

She had the decency not to take refuge in the screen. "No. Not yet." Somehow she managed to sound both gentle and matter-of-fact. "You see, we haven't yet received the instruction form."

"Back from the next of kin?"

"That's right." She leaned confidingly across the desk. "It often takes a while. Some people want to scatter ashes. Others prefer us to inter them. It can take time to come to a decision. We pride ourselves on giving people a bit of a breathing space. And in the meantime there's a secure place where we can keep them."

"For how long?"

She found the question unnerving. "We try not to harry people. We send the odd reminder. And if the form still hasn't come back after a certain time . . ." She made the vaguest gesture towards the arched window looking over the grounds. "We have a nice place out by the north wall."

She didn't add, "In the shadow of that old biscuit factory," but I knew where she meant. Better, I supposed, taking a detour in that direction on my way out, than being left in a box on a shelf in their storage room for eternity. But still, thin comfort for the only one who ever loved you.

That was the week I started to bring home extra work. I didn't want Dana or Audrey to know, and even Mr Hanley would have expected some sort of explanation. So I took to slipping the more complicated of our clients' files into a capacious bag, smuggling them home and then back in the morning.

And still I didn't mention the death at work. I was embarrassed. Embarrassed! They were kind people so they hovered and probed. "Lois, you look very pale." "You seem distracted. Something on your mind?"

Yes. Janie Gay. The house. The life he'd lived. The state that he'd been in. All of the things I'd so determinedly not thought about while Malachy was alive were causing my mind to unravel. I'm not the sort to let myself slide under without a struggle. And so as weeks turned into months and I still woke each morning feeling as limp as a chewed rag and wretchedly besieged by questions rattling round my head, I gradually hatched the sort of reckless courage you see in parents who will take on gangs, the medical profession, even a government, to learn the truth of how their children died. Except, in my case, of course, it wasn't the death that was haunting me. It was the life.

I made my plans. One Saturday, I forced myself to eat my usual breakfast and drove from Pickstone to the Forth Hill estate. I didn't go as far as Janie Gay's, but parked in a place that I had worked out from the map would offer an uncomplicated getaway. Before I got out, I looked at myself in the mirror — an unremarkable woman with soft brown hair, dressed in a plain skirt and blouse. I rehearsed what I'd told myself over and over to stop myself turning back. This Janie Gay has no idea who you are. You're not in the bubbling red wig you wore at her husband's funeral. She's only seen you looking as you do today once in her life, over a year ago, through a car windscreen.

I set off down the street that led to her house.

It felt like learning to walk. That sounds ridiculous, but as I tried to tell myself "Walk normally," it was as if I'd lost the gift of unthinkingly putting one leg in front of the other. I was no longer even sure what was a sensible pace. Would people look at me and wonder, "Why's *she* in such a hurry?" Or would they think, "She's clearly loitering. Up to no good"?

The house was semi-detached. If you were generous, you'd try to say it wasn't such a far cry — at least in design — from the home in which Malachy was raised. But, oh, the difference from Rosslyn Road! Where we'd had glossy paintwork, Janie Gay's last few grey paint peelings clung to rotting wood. We'd had a tidy bright garden. The patch of grass in front of this house was scuffed to bare earth, fringed by the dying remnants of box hedging, and busy with whirligigs of litter spinning in the breeze. Sun sparkled off our windows. The smears and grime on Janie Gay's glass panes must have seen off the daylight, let alone the sun. The gate — or what was left of it — swung on one hinge.

There was no sign of life behind the grey net curtain pinned across the upstairs window. The front door was ajar. In the dark of the hall I could make out a heap of refuse bags, and hanging from a shelf was —

"Hey, you old fuckbag! Had your eyeful yet?"

I jumped a mile. I hadn't realized how my pace had slowed. And far from being hidden safely away behind her net curtains, Janie Gay had silently come up behind me in the street. Now she was leaning against next door's fence, a cigarette dangling, like some young opera singer practising her pose for Carmen. She looked like a cartoon slattern, but more dangerous.

"Nosy fucking parker. Piss off!"

I forced myself not to run. Act *normal*, I urged myself. Tell her that it's a free country. People can stand in the street and look at other people's gardens. So she can go away *herself*.

Oh, very likely! There I stood, in my neat pleated skirt and sensible shoes. And I have never in my life been rude to any stranger. I started twittering. "I am so sorry. I didn't realize that this was your house. You see, I heard a noise — like a small animal in pain. Or maybe a baby crying . . ."

"Oh, *fuck!*"

Practically shoving me aside, she took off up the path. I saw the packet of cigarettes she'd just slipped out to buy clenched in her hand as she pushed at her door. It swung back further to reveal the baby — wide awake but quiet — strapped in his stroller.

Had he just woken? If not, why wasn't he already howling to find himself abandoned in that dark hall? If I'd left Malachy tethered like that in his pushchair, I would have heard his screams of outrage behind me all the way to the shop and all the way back. Was this child simply used to being left alone? Or did he know there was another person somewhere in the house, ready to pick him up and comfort him if he should panic?

Odd, though, that she'd not taken him along with her. After all, he was dressed. If there had been a struggle to get him into the stroller, it was already over. He was ready to go. And it was a dry bright morning. A bit of fresh air would have done him good — even the couple of moments it might have taken her to get to the end of the street, buy her fresh pack of cigarettes and then come back.

Except I hadn't noticed any shops as I was walking. Curious, I retraced my steps. I reached the corner. Nothing. No shops, no kiosk and no vending machine. A man walked past. The fingers of one hand were stained a fierce yellow. On an impulse I hurried up behind him. "Where is the nearest place I can buy cigarettes?"

"Across the park." He saw my blank look. "Down there. On the right."

I went that way and, sure enough, between two buildings I found an alley with a host of signs forbidding this and that. It opened up into a little park. It wasn't pretty, but there were trees and bushes and plenty of starlings scavenging among the chip wrappers and broken pizza boxes. Certainly it would have *done*. A child in a pushchair takes an interest in anything. Did Janie Gay not realize that, young as he was, her son was all ears, all eyes? Getting on for a year old. At that age you push them to the park to see what's there. You make a fool of yourself in front of strangers and tramps. "Look at the pretty ducks! Quack-quack! Quack-quack!"

The child stares solemnly, as if his ears are stopped with wax. No smile. No happy burbles. No response at all. But, three nights later, when you try to turn the page of the story book, down comes the chubby hand, spread like a starfish to stop you. A thumb's uncorked to free the other hand, and down comes the pointy finger, straight to the crosspatch little duck stamping his feet in the sandpit, or riding her speedboat over the bright-blue waves.

"Quack-quack! Quack-quack!"

Yes, they are listening to every word and watching each flicker of sunlight. Why would you ever leave them strapped in the dark of a hallway on such a morning? And how long had she been away? I'd crossed the park, and there was still no sign of any shop. I asked again. It was around the corner. I checked my watch and timed the walk back. Seven minutes. Four, maybe, at a run but Janie Gay had not been out of breath when she surprised me. And she'd had time to light a cigarette. If she could take time out to be offensive to a passing stranger, how long might she have lingered with friends she met on the way there or back?

So. Better call it ten.

I found the way back to my car. "And don't drive past again," I told myself. "*Ever.* Keep well away. Pretend the Forth Hill estate doesn't exist." A woman my age knows all her limitations, and the last thing in the world that I could bear was for that door to swing ajar again, and show me, strapped forlornly in his stroller in that drab hall, that solemn staring child.

CHAPTER
THIRTEEN

Still, there is duty. And with Malachy gone, and no one coming after me for debts he'd ratted on or deals he'd left undone, there seemed no reason not to get in touch with Mrs Kuperschmidt. I thanked her for her letter all those months ago. She asked about the funeral. I told her I was too upset to go, and she passed on a little of what the police officer who attended had told her after: "He said it was a very simple service. But someone gave a nice little talk about Malachy. And Janie Gay was very dignified."

It offered me the chance to ask, "And do you know about the baby?"

She sounded guarded. "Know about the baby?"

"If he's all right. If Janie Gay is looking after him."

There was a pause as Mrs Kuperschmidt tried to work out where I was headed. Finally she said, a little distantly, "As far as I'm aware, Lois, the Dewell family isn't on our books."

"Dewell?" I must admit I was startled. "Isn't her name Gay?"

"Janie Gay. Janie Gay Dewell. Lois, I'm gathering you can't have met her properly. And yet you're obviously worried about her baby."

Sensing Mrs Kuperschmidt's unease, I tried to sound robust. "Well, what with my Malachy being tangled up in drug deals, and the police officers seeming to know the child's mother so well, I just assumed that you'd be keeping a weather eye out. At least at the start. Just in case . . ."

I trailed off.

Mrs Kuperschmidt said sternly, "Lois, do you know something you're not telling me?"

"No, no." I stretched the truth, but only a little. "I've never so much as set eyes on this baby." I almost added, "For all I know, he isn't even my son's child," but realized just in time that that would make my phone call sound even more odd.

"So you've no reason to suspect the child's in any danger?"

I was still fishing like mad. "It has to be danger, does it? Before you can step in to take a look?"

Mrs Kuperschmidt was as tactful as she could be in urging caution. "Lois, you know as well as I do these things are subtle. The trouble is that everyone's an expert on other people's kids. So we get calls from neighbours and grandparents — even from absent fathers. We do the best we can. But all too often the problem amounts to little more than —" The phrase she used must have sprung straight from a text book. "— coming at childraising from different cultural reference points."

"You mean, like living on chips? And watching telly day and night? That sort of thing?"

"That sort of thing. And worse. Constantly being sworn at, or squashed or ignored. Cruelly teased, even. There have to be a million horrible ways of raising children without crossing the line. Sometimes we do step in to offer support to the family." She gave a heavy sigh. "But we're so *limited*. It mostly boils down to pulling strings to get a child into a nursery, or giving a bit of advice about feeding it better." Another sigh. "It's not as if the parents haven't been told it all before. They almost always ignore it."

Just being so honest had depressed her utterly. Briskly she tried to wrap up the call to get away from me. "Honestly, Lois. I know you're worried. And if you should ever hear anything specific, we'd move at once to try to put things right. But from what I've heard, Janie Gay might have a temper but she's not vicious. And though by all accounts she won't win any natty housekeeping awards, she's certainly not incapable. If you'd already been a large part of this baby's world there might have been some tack that we could take. But, in the circumstances —"

Mrs Kuperschmidt took a deep breath. "I hate to say it, Lois, but since there's nothing you can do to change this baby's home background, the best advice that I can give you is to be grateful you and the child weren't close."

Now I was keener than Mrs Kuperschmidt to end the call. What's "close" got to do with it? When I was in hospital losing my very first baby, a woman in a soft grey suit appeared on the ward. My bed was nearest the door. I watched her glance at the clipboard she was carrying, then tuck it under her arm and stroll to a bed at the end. She introduced herself, pulled up a chair, then, at a gesture of consent from the young woman propped against the pillows, tugged the privacy curtain around them. She was there long enough for me to forget about her. Ten minutes? An hour? I was in no state to pay attention. Next time I noticed her she was pulling a chair up close to the patient in the bed beside me and stretching out a hand to tug the flowery cotton curtain across to close the gap between us.

She flashed me a smile that meant nothing. "You don't mind?"

"No. Go ahead."

But I could not go deaf. And all I could assume was that these two patients' treatment could at some time in the future, if they gave permission, include the "harvesting" of eggs for other, infertile women. This time the lady with the clipboard didn't get far through her pitch. If she was on the verge of offering a host of assurances, I never got to hear them. All that came through the curtain was my neighbour's strained voice.

"Let's get this right. You're asking me if I'll donate my *eggs*." She cut off the woman's discreetly murmured response. "You want me to let someone else have a child that's half mine — half mine! — and go through the whole of the rest of my life not having the faintest idea who's looking after it, or what a pig's ear they might be making of the job?" Did the voice shoot higher, or was it simply that the whole of the rest of the ward had fallen silent? "I'm supposed to lie in bed at night and wonder if, out there, some child of mine I'll never know is cold, or crying, or being tormented by some bully?"

Now she was shrieking. "Listen to me, you stupid, stupid woman! Next time you go down a ward asking strangers to offer you eggs, try a test question first. Ask, 'Have you ever in your whole life thought for a moment that you could hand a baby of your own out for adoption?' And if the answer's 'No', then have the sensitivity to skip that person's bed out!"

The hapless visitor was backing off. I could see the bulge in the curtain. "Find someone else!" my neighbour snapped. "Find someone with no children. Or no heart. Or no imagination!"

The fuss was over and the lady in the grey suit fled. But later that day I saw the other patient she'd been talking to first, at the far end, beckon the nurse. There was a flurry of tears. Again the curtain was drawn, and I could only guess that the words spat out so angrily at my end of the ward had taken root and made a difference at the other.

In those days I'd no reason to give the matter much more thought. Why would it interest me, a woman who'd lost, not just her unborn child, but also any confidence she'd ever be pregnant again? Only when Malachy was lying safely in my arms did those hissed words come back to set me thinking. She was so *right*, that woman. She *knew*. I, who could hardly bear to leave my son for half an hour, would have gone mad to think a child of mine was somewhere I didn't know, with someone I couldn't be certain would care for him as well as I would.

And now the thought of it was back again, to haunt my days and nights. The strange small feeling of unease I'd first had driving home after the funeral hardened and sharpened until I realized what it was. Even back then I'd wanted to know what would happen to the baby. It was a small thought when it first began. But it took root and spread, sending its tendrils all over. When you've a dog, you notice other dogs. The same with cats. And people. Hobble out of hospital in bright fresh plaster and suddenly all around, coming out of nowhere, are people on crutches and sticks. And after your missed period and the first sight of that unwavering blue line, you notice every pregnant woman. After the birth, you see nothing but prams and pushchairs, and shops you'd never even noticed on your street turn out to have been there for years, selling things for small children.

And now, wherever I looked, I could see babies. Don't get me wrong. I didn't *want* the baby. I simply wanted to know he'd be all right. After all, the chances were that he was my grandchild — the only one I'd ever get to have. I *hated* to think about him being raised by Janie Gay. Oh, she might not be bad enough to bring the social services down on her, but you could tell, simply from looking, she'd be the sort to have the television on like moving wallpaper from morning till night. She'd not speak to the child except to scold him. And she'd be far too idle to make a fair distinction between bad behaviour and the simple restlessness of a toddler bored to the limit and beyond.

No. She'd be a shouter and a secret slapper. And all her concern and interest and attention would stay fixed firmly on herself. I knew her sort — one of those ghastly women so proud of their emotions they leak them out to swamp the rest of us. They think we want to know about their endlessly unruly feelings — even assume we'll admire them. I didn't have to talk to Janie Gay to know what she'd be like. I had seen people like her on all those vulgar television shows. "I love him to *bits*," they say of the child they're always so happy to ignore, or blame and punish. "I'm *gutted!*" they go round wailing whenever the shoes they take a fancy to in the shop window are out of stock in their size.

I wasn't raised like that. Neither was Malachy. And yet that little soul staring forlornly from the gloom of that hallway faced a whole childhood of it. I couldn't bear the thought. Up until now, my own determined ignorance of what was going on had been a comfort I had rested on like a soft pillow.

Now my brief tangle with Janie Gay had shredded it, the worries spun like feathers round my head.

I had ignored the problem long enough. Something would have to be done.

CHAPTER
FOURTEEN

Easy things first. Over the next few days I filled a large plastic laundry tub with second-hand toys just right for a child of his age. I rummaged happily through charity shops each lunch time and on Saturday morning. There were some real finds. I was continually astonished at the high quality of things I managed to unearth, and their low prices. I bought a bear on wheels, a complicated but sturdy garage with ramps and a carwash area, an inspection pit and even a little working wind-up lift to the car park on top. I found a set of jigsaws on a farm-animal theme. Someone had taken the trouble to draw a symbol on the back of each little wooden piece so, though the colours of all three pictures were similarly bright, it would be easy to sort the bits into the right boxes whenever they got muddled.

Just in case, I threw in a small selection of the sort of toys that any baby in a normal home would have already: an interesting rattle, a cuddly owl, a box of bricks and bright plastic rings stacked on a cone. I found a good jack-in-the-box, and even bought one of those flat plastic affairs designed to hang in the cot that offer a fat round mirror and various buttons to flick or twirl or press to make things spin, or set a nursery tune playing.

That evening, I wrote a note: *Dear Janie Gay, I was just chucking things out and thought you might be able to use these.* After a bit of thought, I signed it "*M*". Janie Gay might scratch her head, but no doubt like the rest of us she lived in a world of Margarets and Michelles, of Megans and Marys, and was unlikely to be suspicious.

Next morning I got up an hour before dawn, loaded the car, and drove to Forth Hill. I parked as close to Janie Gay's house as I dared. There wasn't a soul about, and not a sound, except for odd scatterings of birdsong. First I slid out the large and unwieldy garage. I took great care with Janie Gay's broken gate for fear it would creak and wake her or the baby. Propping the garage against it to hold it open, I went back for the plastic basket, then tiptoed up the path. Not overly trusting her neighbours, I went round the side, out of sight of the street. A motorbike festooned with chains made it quite awkward to get past, and at the back the crumbling concrete path gave way to the scuffed earth of a pocket-handkerchief garden. I put the basket down a step or two before my shadow fell across the window. Suppose she was up? I tucked the note I'd written under one wing of the furry owl, and hurried back to fetch the garage. Then I slipped away, feeling as cheery and triumphant as any bank-robber after the perfect heist.

Flushed with success, I went back to the charity shop the following week. I can't really say what I was after this time. More toys? A sailor hat? Some bedtime-story books? But from the moment I walked through the door I saw what I wanted. It was propping open the door to the stockroom: a padded child's safety seat — one of the sort that fits in any make of car.

I lugged it over to the woman behind the sales desk. "How much is this?"

She said she couldn't sell it. It was their policy, she explained. No second-hand electrical goods, no helmets and no car seats. "Just in case."

"Just in case what?"

"In case they don't work properly." Her tone of voice made her contempt for such a jobsworth policy perfectly plain. "In case they're 'compromised', they tell us. No longer 'fit for the purpose'."

"So what's it doing here," I asked her, "tempting a browser like me?"

"It was left in the doorway along with a heap of other stuff that was there when we opened."

"Oh, right."

The other Lois would have left the matter there — felt a bit irritated as she walked away, and forgotten before she reached the corner. But there was a new Lois now — a bold, uncaring Lois who could be conjured out of me as easily as a wig can be lifted from a box. I drove straight home, and changed out of my blouse and skirt into a pair of slacks and a smart sweater. I tugged on the wig, put on the glasses that I'd worn to the funeral, and drove straight back.

Here was a test. This time I wasn't sneaking into a shadowy chapel at the last minute. I stood in the full

98

light of the charity-shop window facing a woman I'd talked to less than an hour before.

She didn't blink.

Neither did I. "I am so sorry!" I gushed. "You see, this morning, by mistake, my husband left our grandchild's car seat with a heap of stuff I'd asked him to drop off on his way to —"

I didn't even finish. Already she'd interrupted, expressing her delight that the car seat had found its way home. She threaded her way between the over-stuffed racks towards the storeroom at the back, still cheerfully chatting. "We couldn't have sold it anyhow. And it's not as if the things are cheap. My daughter-in-law recently had to buy one, and I was shocked at how much she had to pay."

She handed it over, not looking in the least bit puzzled by anything about me. Clearly, once I was in the wig, even my voice became some unobtrusive part of me that wasn't noticed. From sheer relief (not to mention a stab of guilt at getting a perfectly good car seat for nothing) I pressed some money into the donation box and walked out, glowing with triumph.

It was so *easy*, I had realized. Nobody ever looked twice. Curly red hair worked like a mask. It was the only thing that people saw, so you could be a whole new self without a tremor. Is that what gave me the confidence to make the first little visit? For that is how I thought of it: "the little visit". That's even what I called it as I prepared. On the drive to and from work, and in the shower, and wiping down the surfaces after my supper, I would run practise conversations through my head, imagine all sorts of scenarios. I faced the fact that Janie Gay might be in any sort of mood from indifferent to virulent. (I somehow couldn't imagine her being *nice*.) I tried to think how I would deal with any line she took. I worked out all the lies I might be pushed to tell. And, bearing in mind the temper that caused her to lash out at Malachy under the bridge all that long time ago, I even warned myself over and over to make sure that, whatever happened, I had the sense to stay between her and the door.

And then I took an afternoon off work. ("Good on you, Lois. Doing something nice?") I drove halfway, pulled on the wig in the privacy of a church car park, then drove on to the estate and walked with confidence up the short pitted path to Janie Gay's front door.

I pressed the doorbell. There was a shuffling noise. I pictured Janie Gay burying her feet into a pair of furry high-heeled mules and scowling ("Oh, for heaven's sake! What is it *now*?"), and nearly lost my nerve. But it was too late to turn back.

The door was opened by the very same floppy-haired lad who'd led the way to this same house after the funeral.

"Sssh! Don't wake Larry."

At last! If I did nothing more than turn and flee I would have managed something. I would have learned the baby's name. Larry.

The boy was eyeing me rather as if he too might be remembering that we'd seen one another before. I felt a stab of nerves, but even before I had the time to say another word he'd opened the door wider. "Janie Gay's not here. But I suppose you'd better come in."

It sounded a good deal more fatalistic than welcoming, but still I stepped in the hallway. He put out a hand to push open the door to the living room, then clearly thought better of that and went on to the kitchen. It was a whole lot cleaner and brighter than I'd imagined — tidy even, apart from a mouldering armchair jammed in the corner and the clutter of toys on the floor. I recognized the stacking bricks and loops of different colours, and felt my first ever wash of warmth for Janie Gay. At least she hadn't thrown them out.

And then I heard the squawk and noticed the cot in the corner. "Oh!"

The boy was grinning. "Nobody sees him till he makes a noise. But it's a whole lot warmer down here than in that bedroom. I put that board up so he can't get splashed from the oven. But sometimes, when he's asleep, even I can forget that he's in here."

The squawk had turned into a determined wail. The boy reached over to scoop up the baby. Larry.

Instantly the wailing stopped, and with the baby nestling against him, the young man temporarily seemed to forget that I was there as he soothed Larry. "Had a good long nap? Want some milk? *Course* you do. There's my boy. Who's a clever old thing?" The whole time he was chuntering away, he was using his free hand to dig in a cupboard for a saucepan, then reach in the fridge. He discarded one carton. "No, that's not your milk, is it, Larry boy? Yours is the proper stuff, isn't it? There we go. Not long now. Just hang on a moment while Daddy warms it."

Daddy? Could that be true? Of course it was always possible, knowing what little I did of people Janie Gay's age and their lives. And what a great relief that would turn out to be. But on the other hand, the word might mean nothing. I thought back to something one of Malachy's teachers told me once, in an attempt to console me after some misdemeanour of my son's that had filled me with shame: "He's in with a challenging bunch of boys, Mrs Henderson. A lot of them lack stability. Do you know, walking behind a pair of them yesterday, I even heard one saying to the other, as casually as you like, 'You've got my old dad now, haven't you?' What do you think about that?"

So maybe this was indeed my real and only grandson, and this was his very first "new dad" so deftly pouring the milk one-handed into the pan, and lighting the gas by striking the match along the edge of the box tucked under his chin. I watched him dip in a finger to check the chill was off the milk, hold up the empty bottle against the light to make sure it was clean, then pour.

Before the bottle was even halfway full, the baby was reaching to grab it. "You need three hands," I told him. "Can I help?" He held out the bottle and I twisted the top in place. The baby snatched it with both hands, and together they fell in the armchair, looking the picture of comfort, the boy with his feet sprawled and Larry curled in his arms.

And then the boy turned towards me. His whole demeanour changed.

"So," he said coldly. "Who are you after? Me — or Janie Gay?"

"After?"

"Oh, don't play games! I'm good on faces. I recognize you from poor old Mally's funeral. We had you sussed even back then. You have to be some sort of police nark."

I don't know what came over me, I really don't. I'd wasted all those hours inventing stories about starting a local playgroup, wanting to know if Janie Gay would answer a survey on shopping patterns, or asking if she had seen my missing dog.

And what came out?

"Nonsense!" I snapped. "I'm not a police officer. Nor some undercover agent or part of the drug squad. I was at Malachy's funeral because I'm a social worker and Malachy was on my files. Now I've moved areas, into child health, and so I'm here to check that Laurence has reached his first-year developmental milestones."

"Milestones?"

"You know. What he can do. And what he can't."

Was the defensive look clearing? "Really? That's all you're here for?"

Oh, I was on a roll. "Didn't you get the appointment card? That tells you what it's all about."

He looked a little shamefaced. "Sorry. Didn't see that."

"Well, never mind. It's perfectly simple. If Janie Gay's not here, I'll just go through things with you." I started scrabbling in my bag for a pen. "So, just to get things straight, you're . . .?"

"Me? My name's Guy."

Who would have thought I had it in me?

"And I'm Mrs Kuperschmidt."

CHAPTER
FIFTEEN

You wouldn't believe what you can learn in half an hour when you've a smiling and cooperative baby and a relieved young man. I must have left that house the most satisfied grandmother on earth. Laurence could walk. He could say "Dada" and "milk" and "more" and "no" and "munny" (for monkey; there was no sign of my cuddly owl). With lots of encouragement he could do a fairly neat job of clapping his hands together and waving goodbye. He could run cars up and down the plastic ramps of his garage.

And he was cosy as toast with his new Dada. When I was leaving ("Well, that's all *splendid*, Guy. Nothing to worry about at all") he clung to his protector's legs and stared at me with those enormous eyes.

"Will you be back?"

I hedged my bets. "Somebody will," I said. "For the next milestone check. It might not be me, of course."

"Shame," he said, with only the statutory tinge of sarcasm I guessed a young man of his sort would feel obliged to show to anyone in authority. I walked out with that feeling of exhilaration you get from realizing you've done exactly the right thing at the exact right time. The child was fit and happy. The boy was a born father — better, I had to admit to myself, than Malachy would ever have been. During our unofficial interview I had found out that he was born in Dover, had a string of sisters younger than himself, a mother with three separate jobs, and he'd moved north to work in a stables. (In spite of the motorbike cluttering the side path, it was, it seemed, horses that were his passion.) Then he'd been sacked. I didn't learn the details, but sensed it might be something to do with petty theft. He had run into Janie Gay on a night out, and though he never said as much, I had the feeling he'd been on the scene before my Malachy. Now he was back again.

And I was grateful. Frankly, I could have turned and hugged him at the door. Now I could walk away, shrug off the pall of worry hanging over me, and get on with my life. I could —

But what, exactly? Water the plants in my arbour? Sit at my desk and stare out at herons and swallows? No. Something about the rush of relief that I'd been feeling must have taken hold. Restlessness spread. Instead of going home, I drove to the canal and walked along the path — not to where Malachy drowned; I went the other way, through the park scarred with signs and past converted mills. Something was shifting inside me. I felt different. It was a growing sense of freedom, yes; but much, much stronger than the mere shelving of responsibility.

And then I realized. It was the end of my old life. My long, long convalescence from living with Stuart and raising Malachy was over.

Time to stop sleepwalking and start again.

★ ★ ★

The things I did. Ceramics. Salsa dancing. Italian classes. It was a massive change. I wasn't used to going out, or having fun, or even throwing myself into things with enthusiasm. Always before, there had been something eating away at my soul's edge that spoiled things like that. I probably inherited the feeling. When I looked back, I realized that my parents had never belonged to any clubs or societies — even avoided going to other people's homes. If there was any excuse to turn down an invitation, they wouldn't hesitate to use it. When it was hard to refuse, they put on brave faces but took no pleasure in the prospect. All of my mother's concern fell on to what she should wear, what time they should arrive, how long it would be best to stay and whether or not they should take something with them. (If so, what?) She wouldn't talk about these deep anxieties, but I'd drift home from school and, going up the stairs, see her forlornly staring into her closets, and guess what was on her mind.

By the time the day came, the problem had loomed over her so long she was exhausted. She'd put on whichever skirt and top she had decided was the least unsuitable, and inspect herself in the mirror. There'd be no satisfaction in this appraisal. She might as well have been — and probably was — checking for stains and pulled threads. The faintest sigh would give me to understand she'd passed her own unsmiling test. Then she would turn to my father, and carp at him until he finally looked as close to what she called "right" as they could manage between them. Then off they'd go, as if to their own child's funeral. Brave. Hopeless. This must be *endured*.

When they came back the only mood was of relief. "That wasn't too bad, was it?" "No," — and this added in a tone of guarded astonishment — "I quite enjoyed it. They were very nice."

In my own marriage, things weren't all that different. Unlike my parents, Stuart wasn't ill at ease on social occasions; he simply couldn't be bothered to get involved in them. Throughout the month I might make a string of suggestions. "Shall we invite some people round for a drink?" "Want to go out to eat tonight?" "Perhaps on Friday we could see a film?" He'd shrug. And, rather than face the fact that his sheer lack of response had cast a pall over the notion, I'd tell myself I hadn't been that keen in any case, and let the matter drop. The very few times I did complain that he'd ignored a suggestion, he turned defensive. "I never said I *wouldn't*." Or, "All right, so I didn't bring it up again. But neither did you."

It's not till things change that you realize how they were before. I didn't tell myself, "Lois, it's time to loosen up," but that's what happened. Everything about my life became more cheerful. The people at work noticed the difference in me. Instead of keeping up their habit of discretion, one by one they cracked. "You're looking very merry, Lois. Had a nice weekend?"

And I would tell them. One day I came in cheerful because the Italian lesson of the evening before had done no more than cover trodden ground and I had realized just how far we'd come. The very next morning I heard myself bewailing the fact that for the second week in a row the salsa class lottery had landed me with the partner I'd privately dubbed "Clumsy Claud". I wasn't just more chatty about day-to-day matters. Now I began to let things drop about myself and my life. I wasn't fully honest. But I did gradually let it be known I had a marriage behind me, and a divorce, and mentioned Stuart's cousins in South Africa often enough for Dana and Audrey to assume that's where my husband had gone. I even told them that we'd had a son (they were quite shocked) and left them with the half-truth, "There was a horrible accident and he was drowned." I'm sure they came to think that when I'd first joined them in the office I'd still been eaten up with grief and only now was coming to life again.

Yet it was not "again", but for the very first time. I look back now and I can count them off: the first professional auburn streaks through my hair; the first bright colours in my wardrobe; the first strappy sandals; the first garden lounger (though there was barely room for it to be unfolded in my small arbour); the first solo holiday (Gerona! With waiters patient enough to listen, and charming enough to commend me on my Italian). I even gathered my forces to ask Mr Hanley for my first rise. ("Odd you should mention that, Lois. For some time now I have been meaning to call you in.") And, when I came out, it was mine.

I even had a fling. It was so odd to find myself in bed with a man again. He had the strangest way of wrapping his legs round mine to pull me closer. He certainly gave me pleasure — far more than Stuart. He brought us little treats to eat in bed. He had a fund of very funny jokes, and he was easy company. One evening he came round in tears because he'd learned the family dog had been run over. "Can we watch telly, Lo? It's all I'm fit for tonight."

We watched at least four solid hours of rubbish. "Christ, this is *crap*!" he kept on saying. But whereas Stuart would have managed to make me feel I was to blame for that, Dan said it happily in tones of growing admiration that one show after another could be so poor. The worse they were, the more the two of us began to enjoy them. Just after eleven he picked up his coat. "I'd better be off, Lo. Early start tomorrow. But thanks for a *lovely* evening. I feel a million times better."

I heaped the coffee cups into the sink and went up to bed singing. So when Dan finally admitted how much he felt for me, it was a wrench to have to tell him that we couldn't carry on. I wasn't in the mood to let even a shadow of a guilty feeling back in my life. He was relieved. I begged for one of the photos of his three children mucking about on a beach. The youngest had a port-wine stain across her cheek. ("They'll have a go at it, but not till she's older.") I told him I'd like to keep the photo as a talisman for lonely moments. His children looked so happy, it would remind me of why I'd been so firm in seeing him off.

But after he'd gone, there were no lonely moments. Oh, I had loved his company. But I liked being alone. I don't remember ever feeling bored. The days sailed past. And every few weeks I'd take the time early on Saturday morning to drive to the Forth Hill estate. Sometimes I'd park a little way along the street. When the For Rent sign went up in front of the house across the fence from Janie Gay's, I even took to saving time by driving past slowly, as if I were simply one more house-hunter trying to decide whether to make an appointment to view. A single glimpse of a tall, easy-moving, floppy-haired shadow moving behind the window would be enough for me and I'd be off, back to my plants or my Italian grammar. I didn't even try to fool myself that I was there to look for Larry. No. I was there to check my living, breathing conscience was in place.

Guy. The very sight of him lifted my heart. His loping stride. The way he'd race along the pavement, pushing the stroller at breakneck speed, then stop it dead to send Larry into paroxysms of excitement. "Again! Again!" The way, on bright mornings, he wouldn't bother with the pushchair at all. "No wheels today, Larry boy." He'd brush the raindrops off the motorbike seat, plonk on the toddler for the statutory pretend ride ("Brrrrm-brrrm! Brrrm-brrrrrm"), then lift him off and swing him up on his shoulders as easily as if the child weighed no more than air. He'd grip the chubby legs. Larry would plunge his fingers into the mop of marmalade hair that never seemed to grow longer, and off they'd go, ducking under next door's already leaning For Rent sign, along to the park, or to buy bread, or cigarettes for Janie Gay. I didn't stay to find out. I'd simply lower the map behind which I'd been hiding, a middle-aged woman in a parked car — who'd notice me? — and drive off home. If Larry had Guy to watch over him, all was well with the world.

And then, one February morning, my ministering angel was gone. His bike no longer leaned, dripping with chains, against the garden fence. The lights in the house came on, and when I drove past for the third time, the downstairs curtains had been drawn back at last. But though I sat there for a whole two hours, no one came out. I thought about knocking on the door with some excuse or another, but didn't dare. I went home, spent a sleepless night, and was back first thing in the morning, ready to wait all day if necessary but convinced that Janie Gay would come out some time, if only to buy cigarettes.

And I was right. I'd barely watched the house for half an hour when a fierce rapping on the glass behind caused me to yelp with terror. I spun around. Sure enough, Janie Gay was leering at me triumphantly through the passenger-seat window. Either she'd been out all the time, or she had suddenly noticed me sitting so quietly in my car and left the house by her back door to sneak around behind me through next door's garden.

I'm not a fool. I let the window down less than a hand's breadth.

"Think we're all fucking *blind*?" she spat at me. "Think I'm so fucking thick I don't even notice when someone like you parks on her arse for hours in front of my house? Think I'm too fucking poor to have a phone, or too stupid to use it?"

She was grasping the rim of the window with both hands, working up her temper. I thought the glass might break. She was already too fired up to worry I might tip the control button the other way to send the window up and trap her fingers.

I was in the worst panic. But into my mind came a trace memory of myself storming out in just the same way to accuse Tansy's boyfriend of spying. It gave me an idea. "Don't be so silly," I snapped at Janie Gay. "I'm not even *looking* at your house, except in so far as it's next door to mine."

That rattled her a little. "Yours?"

I pointed at the weather-worn For Rent sign leaning drunkenly against the hedge at Number 144. "Didn't you know? I've just signed a contract. I'm simply sitting here thinking about new colours for the paintwork, and whether to ask the agency to take down that ratty hedge and start again or do what you've done — put up a little fence."

Her fingers slackened on the glass. She drew her face back. I rolled down the window. Leaning across, I offered her a charming smile and stuck my hand out.

"Since we'll be neighbours, then, how do you do?"

CHAPTER
SIXTEEN

Not for a moment did I think of what I said as anything other than a way of getting out of there without a face covered in scratches. I was too rattled to drive. Before I even reached the main road, I'd realized that I was a hazard and pulled into Marriot's supermarket car park to calm down and think. I obviously couldn't watch the house again. Janie Gay wasn't daft. This time she'd stared at me so hard she'd recognize me anywhere. She even knew my voice. I'd underestimated her and I had blown it. Wig or no wig, there was no way I could risk coming back to make sure —

What? That she was bothering to feed Larry properly? Not leaving him alone for hours? Not endlessly slapping and shrieking? I could go back to Sarah Kuperschmidt, but there was nothing new to say. A child of two was living with his mother. The boyfriend had upped sticks and left. No special sob story there. What was it she had said? "There have to be a million horrible ways of raising children without crossing the line." Poor little Larry would have to take his chances.

Unless . . .

No! Absolutely not! I *loved* my little house. I loved my sunny and sweet-smelling arbour. I'd got to know my neighbours just enough to chat over the fence and feed their cats when they were off on holiday. Why would I want to sell up and move to the ghastly Forth Hill estate? I'd never feel safe. My car would have its wing mirrors torn off just about every week. And the very idea of having Janie Gay as a neighbour filled me with horror. I knew her sort — hair-triggered to interpret every word as a slight and make a hobby out of finding fault. Within a week her insults and litter, garden weeds and God knows what else would be making their way through the tumbledown barrier between our two houses. You only had to look at her to know she was the type to all but encourage her offspring to pull down fences and make holes in the hedge, and treat other people's property as if it were merely some extension of their own.

But that, of course, was the *point*. Larry would need a kind heart looking out for him, and who better than someone who appeared to have moved in next door purely by accident but kept her ears pinned back, listening for trouble? A person who would recognize the signs of misery and abuse, and know at once if anyone violent moved in. Someone who, with Guy gone, could stealthily take over the task of watching out for a vulnerable child.

No! It was a step too far. I simply couldn't — dare not, even — think of it. The very idea set me shuddering. But they are strange, the things that push our lives down paths we never would willingly have taken. As I sat fretting in that supermarket car park, I happened to see something that might have been choreographed to change the course of my life. Out through the glass doors came a family. The father pushed a trolley piled almost to overflowing. He had a sour look, as if the time spent wheeling it up and down the aisles had more than taken its toll. The mother pushed an empty stroller. Her face was closed against the world, as if the two of them had just been quarrelling and she was in a sulk. Certainly she paid no attention to any of the pretty little girls with tight-looking topknots in their hair, trailing behind her.

Twice the father turned to order his daughters to catch up. Both times, the elder two jumped to it. Only the smallest — a sweet-looking thing little more than a toddler — kept stubbornly to her own pace.

Words passed between the couple. I couldn't hear, but it was obvious the tone was unpleasant and the man was losing the last of his patience. Suddenly he turned and, abandoning the trolley, wrenched the pushchair out of his wife's hand and marched back, causing the first two daughters to jump aside, until he reached the youngest child.

There he stood, pointing into the stroller. The child kept up her stride. And then, so fast I wondered if I'd really seen it, the man reached out and snatched the child up by her beribboned topknot. Swinging her up, he took his time to shake her in the air above the pushchair, like a rag doll, before he carelessly dropped her into it.

The child's face was a mask of pain, and worst of all was hearing how promptly the poor mite managed to douse her blinding scream.

Sick to my stomach, I sat paralysed. And by the time I had stopped shaking, the decision was made.

It was a dingy office in a row of shops headed for demolition. Some were already boarded up, and only a couple of the shopkeepers who were still trading had bothered to remove their overnight grilles. The boy who jumped to his feet seemed startled to see anyone come through the door. "You're lucky to catch me. This branch is closing next week."

I told him the address: 144 Limmerton Road. He rifled through a drawer in one of his filing cabinets. "The office in Kenton is dealing with all these now. I shouldn't really —" Tugging out the file, he saw the photo of the property and broke off. "Sure you mean this one? Sure you've got the right street?"

"I'm sure."

He named the rent. I didn't think that I'd grown up wrapped in cotton wool, but still it had never occurred to me that anything that had a roof on it could be leased out for such a small amount. "Sorry?"

The boy was grinning. "You'd have to pay the council tax, of course. And the utilities."

"Still —"

He couldn't contain his amusement. "I know! It's just a heap of beans. It's all coming back to me now. Some old boy rented the place for years, until his landlord started dickering on about wanting to sell it.

One of the old man's two sons stepped in, put down the cash and bought it for his father. He even registered the house in his father's name. Then the old geezer pops his clogs, of course. No one can find a will, so now the son who contributed nothing is grasping for his share. Our client's contesting, of course. But meanwhile he's happy to do anything he can to spite his brother — won't sign for any repairs so we can charge a proper rent — 'Happy to let it *rot*,' — that sort of thing." The grin was widening. "You've seen it."

"Actually, I haven't."

"Well, I can tell you this. You're definitely not going to want it." But he was clearly in the mood to take a break from clearing out the office. "Want to take a look? We'll go in your car, then it won't get scratched or kicked about while we're gone and I won't have to feel guilty."

All the way there, he pointed at things through the window like an excited child. "See that burned-out bike? . . . Look! An Alsatian! . . . The pattern on that woman's coat could scare off crows." I couldn't even remember when I had last had someone in the passenger seat whose company I so enjoyed. I was quite sorry when we drew up outside.

Mercifully, there was no sign of Janie Gay inside her own house as we went up next door's path. The door swung open to the most appalling smell of damp and yet another cheery remark from my companion. "That stink will take some shifting. I doubt if any of the heaters have been switched on since the old fellow was carried out in his box."

I felt a tremor of unease. "How long ago was that?"

"Oh, quite a while. There's been another tenant since, but we could never get hold of him. I think he spent all of his time at his girlfriend's." He pushed open the door to the kitchen. "And who can blame him?"

Certainly not me. The place was a tip. Curtains of black mould sheeted up the walls. Wallpaper peeled down. The ancient vinyl floor was cracked and pitted. Tidemarks of grease flared round the oven. In every room lay broken bits of furniture, and it was clear that, before the damp had finally driven them away, even the spiders had been confident enough to spin their webs from the unshaded bulbs.

"I'll take it."

The boy laughed. "It is shocking, isn't it?"

"No, really. I'm serious. I'll take it."

He looked appalled. "You *can't*. This isn't any place for someone like you. I mean, you could be my —"

He broke off, horribly embarrassed at having so nearly compared me with his own mother, who wouldn't live there in a thousand years. Knowing how quickly surprise would turn into suspicion, I offered him the simplest explanation I could think of for why a woman like me might want to rent a place like this. "There's someone I'd quite like to give the slip — just till things calm down a little." I toyed with the clasp of my handbag. "You know . . ."

The world is stuffed with men who won't accept that a woman wants to leave. The boy was on the case at once and nodded. "Gotcha!"

I turned my honest face towards him. "This is the last place on earth I can imagine him expecting to find me."

"Not half!"

"And after what I've been through . . ."

He said as gallantly as if I truly had been his own mother, "Your secret's safe with us. We make a point of never divulging any private information at all about our clients."

If I'd not taken to him quite so much, I might have laughed in his face.

So you could argue that the gods were kind. I went into that office prepared to say goodbye for ever to my little house and arbour, and live in exile. Now, with a bit of scrimping and a readjustment of the loan, I'd have two places. One of the things about doing other people's tax returns is that you learn which builder slaps on any old charge he can, and who's as frugal in his invoicing as in his life. I phoned one of our clients — seemingly out of the blue — and his replacement of a few missing roof tiles and a cracked downpipe went a long way to sorting out the damp. Neat bleach dealt with most of the mould. The rest got painted over. I carpeted the floors in offcuts that were going cheap, and rooted through charity shops for sturdy curtains that would stop the draughts round the ill-fitting windows. At the next auction I paid a ludicrously small amount for some quite decent furniture. I didn't worry that none of it matched, telling myself I'd only be there over weekends. A day here, a day there. Simply to keep an eye on things. It wouldn't be too awful.

In less than six weeks, I was in.

CHAPTER
SEVENTEEN

It is a mystery to me how I can ever have become so fond of such a ghastly young woman as Janie Gay. For she was truly *horrible*. Theatrically volatile, chronically steeped in self-pity and childishly spiteful, she had a blinding need to interpret the whole world entirely in terms of herself. No neighbour ever just happened to walk past her house on their own mission. Rather, it was to annoy her by glancing over the hedge and in through her windows. Shops didn't close because the owner could no longer make a living. No, it was to make Janie Gay's life more awkward. Even the street-cleaning schedule hadn't been arranged the way it had simply by accident. The rubbish trucks came early just to wake her up. And there was to be no argument. Janie Gay was unbudgeably convinced that she was right about everything. All disagreement was perceived as a personal attack.

I'd sensed how dangerous she was right from the start and hadn't gone to all that trouble to rent an extra house, and furnish it, to fall at the first hurdle. I was all eyes, all ears. I'd guessed from the almost belligerent way she stood in her own doorway that she wasn't the sort to accept favours. Suspicion ran too deep. If, that first time, I'd made the error of smiling over the fence and saying something along the lines of "You seem to have your hands full. I'd be delighted to babysit the little chap for you at any time," her face would have shut like a trap and I'd have heard her muttering, deliberately loudly, "You stick to your own damn house. Don't try to weasel your way in mine."

I took a different tack. The second weekend I was there, I listened to her snarls and Larry's howls reach one of their crescendos, and snatched up a basket of unwashed cleaning cloths to give me the excuse to rush outside. Tossing the first few over the washing line as I pretended I couldn't hear the poor child's desperate wailing, I called to Janie Gay casually over the fence, "See your boy? Mind if I borrow him some time?"

She broke off jerking him this way and that, trying to release some zipper that had jammed. Despite herself, she was intrigued. "Borrow this whiny little bugger? Why would you want to do that?"

"He's the same size as my nephew Sandy and I want to buy some dungarees."

Her nod was almost sympathetic. "Size labelling for kids' stuff is crap."

I was determined to show her that, on this issue at least, we sailed under much the same colours. I cranked up the sort of grinding negativity I knew would appeal to her. "It's only so you end up buying more. Same with that stupid business of pink for girls and blue for boys. It's the big shops that push it. You have a second child and chances are you can't pass anything on."

Hoping I'd proved my credentials as a proper sourpuss, I waved a hand towards Larry. "So can I borrow him? Just for a little while?"

It wasn't in her not to take advantage of some fool who didn't know the price and value of an hour's peace. "Yes, you can have him. Do you want him now?"

I dropped the last few pegs back in the basket. "Now would be wonderful."

On went her bargaining hat. "The thing is, I have to go out soon myself."

"That's perfect, then. It will suit both of us."

"Not sure when I'll be back."

"I'll just hang on to him, then, shall I? Until you're home?"

"You can't use this house. I've got no spare key."

"That's not a problem. He can come back here. If he gets hungry I can give him tea."

The deal was done. I couldn't help but notice she gave me no instructions for Larry's benefit, only advice for my own. "If he keeps bawling, you could try shoving that stupid sucky rag he likes so much back in his face."

"I'll try to remember that."

And I was off with Larry, down to the nearby park, and then, fearing she might come past and spot us, on to the next, half a mile further along. I kept up a stream of chatter and, each time we stopped at a kerb, leaned my head over so the poor mite could get used to the idea that it wasn't his mother pushing him. He didn't seem to care. Still making a puddle of the sticky cake she'd shoved in his hand to quieten him, he was absorbed in everything around us, pointing out each dog and quite unable to settle till I'd agreed, "Yes, it's a doggie."

He seemed a little startled when, at the play park, I stopped to undo his safety clasp. But he scrambled out of the pushchair hastily enough. He wasn't steady on his feet over the humpy verge surrounding the climbing frames or even, for a little while, on the strange spongy safety surface beneath the slides. Clearly since Guy had left he hadn't spent nearly as much time as usual mucking about in parks. But he was soon on form, rushing from one thing to another, clambering up the rocket, hurling himself down the slide, demanding "Higher! Higher!" on the swings.

I kept my eye on the time. I could stay out till three at least, I reckoned, knowing from experience that when a small child's out of the house, the hours fly past. I would have taken the chance to rush round cleaning and tidying or paying a few bills. I didn't think that Janie Gay was the type to be bothered about getting on top of things. God alone knew where she'd go, or what she might be doing.

All the way home, I ran through the plan I'd made to tempt the little chap into a level of confidence that meant he would be willing to come again. I'd stored the usual temptations in my kitchen: those chocolate finger biscuits children of his age adore. Tinned fruit. (I didn't think he would be used to fresh.) Ice cream in several flavours. Even, in case of desperation, sweets.

But once we were through the door, I swung into action. First I made toast. I cut the warm browned slices into tiny squares and spread each one with something different. Within a couple of minutes Larry was staring in wonder at a pretty plate of bite-sized pieces, each with a different topping: peanut butter, Marmite, marmalade, honey, ham, chicken spread, fish paste and cheese.

We made a game of it.

"Nice?" I pointed to the little piece of card on which I'd drawn a smiley face, then to the grumpy one. "Or nasty?"

He pushed the fish paste straight to the nasty side and reached for the cheese. That went down well, so none of it was left to put on either little cartoon. And on he ploughed, industriously tasting, rejecting the Marmite with a look of shock, stuffing the piece of toast with chicken spread into his mouth so fast I wondered where it had gone when I turned back from putting on the kettle.

We did drinks, too. Milk. Orange. Grapefruit (not a great success). Hot chocolate. Fizzy water. While he was sipping, he took to idly fingering a little silver ring that I was wearing. Up until then, I'd held him, carried him, and even given him a kiss and cuddle when he unnerved himself by tumbling too fast from the slide. But this was the first time he had reached out to touch me, and it was a shock. I had forgotten the gentle, tentative patting of chubby fingers.

Enough, I told myself. His eyelids drooped. I scooped him off the little booster seat and carried him through to the sofa. How strange it was, after so many years, to hold a sleeping child. At first, I found myself scouring his face, as I'd been doing all the afternoon, for any look of my own son. Soon I was lost in regret. Why hadn't I had the sense to realize, when Malachy was this age, that just the chance to hold soft limbs and trace a finger over the scabs on a knee is something precious? Back then, a smear of marmalade across a cheek was simply one more thing to be wiped off. Now, all these years later, it was one more chance to run a finger over skin so smooth it could be porcelain. How stupid to have been so very busy all through Malachy's childhood. The cleaning, cooking, shopping — even going to the park became a chore. Back then, I'd always tip the sleeping child out of my arms into his cot with a great sigh of relief. How many hours had I missed of simple pleasure? Our troubles always come at the wrong time. But so, I realized with a pang, do gifts.

She wasn't back until well after seven. I heard the screech of brakes a few yards up the street and, glancing out, saw a small blue car reversing so fast I feared for my own wing mirror. A door swung open and out stumbled Janie Gay, clutching a package and sharing one last laugh with the invisible driver. The car roared off. Janie Gay turned. Her eyes fell on her own house and, like the moment in a pantomime when the clock chimes the last stroke of twelve and, with a flash of light and a puff of smoke, the ballgown changes back to rags and the enchanting princess becomes a kitchen skivvy once again, the contented young girl in front of me turned back into a sour young woman. I watched her plodding up the path as though back into prison and, after the light came on in her kitchen, felt enough sympathy to give her a further hour before I even thought of carrying the faintly snoring Larry down my short path and up hers.

There she stood, in the doorway, fag in hand. "You did all right then?"

"He was fine the whole time. Absolutely fine."

"I meant with the *dungarees*."

All sympathy drained away, to be replaced by my refreshed contempt for her indifference to her child. "Oh, yes. The dungarees." I took the chance to plan a few improvements to Larry's pitiful wardrobe. "Well, better than all right, really. There was a two-for-one sale, so I bought one or two things for Larry as well. I'll bring them round tomorrow."

She'd still not put down her cigarette to take her son from my arms, so I stepped in and looked around. "Where shall I —?"

"There," she said, pointing to the ancient armchair in which, all those months ago, I'd watched him nestling so comfortably on Guy's lap. I laid him down, and realized from the way she was already reaching for the grubby blanket draped over the back of the chair that — so long as he didn't slip off on to the floor — it was where he'd be staying till morning.

That's when I saw the letter. It was underneath the chair. I'd been through the crematorium gates often enough to recognize their crest on the headed paper. I picked it up and glanced at it just long enough to see that it was yet another reminder that she had still to decide what was to be done with her late husband's ashes.

I held it out to her. "Need this?"

"No," she said. "No, that's just rubbish."

I truly think, if Larry hadn't been curled in a ball on that soft armchair peacefully lost in sleep, I would have had a go at throttling her. Rubbish? My own son? Certainly I would have pulled her hair out in great handfuls. As it was I kept my temper, casually affecting to crumple the piece of paper as I turned to her bin.

Keeping my back to her, I tucked the letter away, under my top, and let the bin lid fall.

"Right, then," I told her. "I'll be off."

I waited, fool enough to think that she might thank me for caring for her son for so many hours. Nothing. But, what the hell? She'd had an afternoon's free day care and I had snatched the chance to steal my own son's ashes.

Too much to ask for manners. Deal enough.

CHAPTER
EIGHTEEN

Wherever she'd been, she must have had a really good time because I found it easy enough after that day to wheedle my way into their lives. I'd see her tugging at the pushchair and then at Larry — "For Christ's sake! Get in the bloody thing!" — and snatch up some plant pot, screwdriver or peg basket — any excuse to step out of my own door.

"Want me to watch him?"

I'd stand and wait as the temptation to be rid of Larry for a few hours battled with her determination never to admit that anyone was doing her a favour. Finally she'd think of some way to twist the offer round. "I suppose you want to take him to see that aunt of yours. The one in Pickstone."

"I probably would, yes, if you don't mind him being away a while."

"She really likes him, doesn't she?"

"She really does."

"Oh, all right. Since you're so *keen*. He's a bit mucky."

"I'll sort him out. There are some clothes of Sandy's on the ironing board."

So off we'd go, to see the mythical aunt who lived in Pickstone. I hung a swing in the arbour. I bought a heap of toys and paints and modelling clay for days it rained. I filled a shelf with big bright picture books. I even introduced him to all my neighbours as my grandson Laurence. I'd feed him a decent meal, then strap him in the car seat I'd pounced on all those months ago, and drive him home. There, with the help of the equally non-existent Sandy and all his "outgrown" clothes, I gradually managed to replace the socks so small they cramped poor Larry's toes, the underpants that left ribbed rings around his thighs, and the thin nylon jacket in which he'd spent most of the winter shivering.

I even took him to the crematorium. That was the day I went to fetch the ashes. The wheels had finally turned. I'd carefully flattened the form that Janie Gay had carelessly tossed aside, then ironed the back till it looked good as new. I'd filled in each section, printed my own name and the address in Pickstone inside the space entitled "Named Recipient", then made an excellent stab at forging the indifferent widow's pitifully childish signature before posting it back.

Less than a fornight later a letter came from the crematorium reminding me of office hours and warning me I'd need identification to pick up "the consignment". I took Larry with me only because, when I came out of the house on that Saturday morning, I'd seen him forlornly sitting on the step in his pyjamas.

"Mummy not up yet?"

Larry shook his head.

I went down my path just to walk up hers and push the back door open. "Janie Gay?"

Nothing.

I called up the stairs. "I'm taking Larry for a little while. Is that all right?"

Still not a word. I looked around for some clue as to why she was sleeping so soundly but, though the usual clutter lay all round, there were no bottles. Hoping I wasn't taking too much of a risk with our precarious relationship, I left a note and hurried Larry back next door to dress and feed him.

Then we were on our way. The only parking space was at the far end of the crematorium grounds. Larry was full of beans, leaping from one flat sunlit plaque set in the grass to the next, and having to be persuaded not to uproot the plastic flowers from their mock marble vases. As we reached the older part of the grounds we both became more sober, Larry cowed into good behaviour by the shadow of the ancient cypresses, and me by thoughts of what I was about to do.

We turned the corner in the drive and reached the office. I handed over the stamped release form I'd been sent, along with my proof of identity. Promptly the woman vanished, and came back only a couple of minutes later carrying a carton.

"The cask itself is inside this," she said, almost too hastily, as if she thought I might immediately begin to complain about the quality of the packaging.

What did I care? My knees were trembling. All I could think about was getting out of there. I signed my name so shakily I thought she might become suspicious. But no. She gave me one of those deeply professional looks of sympathy, and patted my hand. I wasn't fooled. I was quite sure she did the same thing half a dozen times a day, almost as part of the package, but still I had to turn away as fast as possible so I could usher Larry to the door before my tears fell.

I looked at my watch. It was no later than half past ten, and I was shattered. "Want to go home?" I asked Larry.

He nodded eagerly. "Want to go on the swing!"

There was no swing at Janie Gay's. He meant the house at Pickstone. On any other day I might have relished this small first proof that, if home is where the heart is, all of my efforts so far had been worthwhile. But with that neatly packaged carton on the passenger seat beside me, I couldn't help but have another boy far closer to mind. So, buying off Larry's disappointment with one of the brightly coloured windmills on a stick that were for sale, along with flowers, at the booth at the main gate, I took him back to Limmerton Road.

Janie Gay met us at the door. Clearly she'd only just woken. With her sleep-softened face and wearing a short shiny nightdress she looked more like an older sister of Larry's than any mother. Her eyes fell on her son. Maybe because I'd had to push him forward towards her, she thought that I'd come to tell tales. Scraping her fringe back from her eyes, she glared at both of us. "What time is it, for heaven's sake! And what's the little sod been up to *now*?"

"Nothing," I told her. "I think the door banged closed behind him and he didn't want to wake you up, so he came round to me."

She ticked him off for leaving the house in the first place, then made it clear she didn't want him back by telling me, "Well, you can keep him if you want."

"Actually, today's not —"

"Otherwise I'm going to have to take him with me."

It sounded almost like a threat. "Where?" I asked.

"Just to a friend's place. But there's nothing for him to do there. And anyway, this person's not at all keen on having kids about." She glanced at Larry and shrugged. "Oh, never mind. I suppose it won't matter." Then, in a tone that made it only too clear that if Larry knew what was best for him, he wouldn't argue, she said to him, "You *like* Uncle Wilbur, don't you?"

Wilbur? How many Wilburs are there in the world?

I took Larry's hand again. "No, it's all right. I'll keep him."

On the way back down the path, I thought this might be just the moment to strike a bargain. "In fact, do you mind if I keep him overnight? You see my aunt in Pickstone is having a party. And she'd particularly like —"

I didn't even need to carry on.

"Whatever! I feel like crap."

"So I could bring him back tomorrow evening?"

She was already halfway through closing the door.

So that's how it came about that I had one young boy at my side when I went off to tip the ashes of another into the sluggish water of the city canal. I'd thought of going to the sea. But for the life of me I couldn't think of any beach I could associate with Malachy. Some people throw the ashes of the ones they love off clifftops or mountainsides. As far as I could recall, Malachy had never so much as climbed up a steep slope without a litany of complaints. If we'd still lived in Rosslyn Road, I could at least have buried the ashes under the sandpit in which I remembered him spending so many happy, busy hours. But this is not a favour you ask of strangers. And so, the longer I sat companionably on the rug with Larry and ran the few last possibilities through my mind, the more clear it became that there were only two places in the world with which, for the rest of my life, I would associate Malachy and have him always, *always* come to mind.

One was the bench on which he'd been sitting the day that the bus to Forth Hill and Danbury came past and swallowed up the two of them.

The other was the towpath as it ran under the stone bridge.

The bus stop was out, of course. But the canal? Why not?

Because the rest of the world would be appalled, simply appalled, to think I'd chosen to tip my own son's ashes into the same dank water in which he'd drowned. And yet, as Larry sat contentedly pounding his little wooden hammer down on the six yellow pegs, then turning the toy to bash them down again from the other side, the thought kept hammering through my mind. That is the place. That's where, for the rest of

135

my life, I'll not be able *not* to think of him. To stand under that stone arch, hearing the drips and feeling the dampness settle on my skin is almost to revive him. Until the day I die, that is the one place that will trigger memories, both good and bad, of my son Malachy. That is the place that will for ever bring back the ghost of my dead child.

So that was it. I had decided. And since I knew I could not spend the night in the same house as Malachy's ashes, I had no choice but to get on with things. Now I was glad that Larry would be by my side. He'd be the perfect cover for a canalside walk. What could appear more natural than a small boy and his grandmother under the bridge, bent over the water. If I was spilling something in, it might be the gritty dregs of a goldfish bowl, or some fish dead in a tank. Who would think twice?

Setting the carton on the table, I slit the tape that held the flaps in place and slid out the casket. It was plain and black and, for what I took to be the cheapest standard issue, looked almost sleek. A slim metal label fastened with two pins bore Malachy's name. I prised it off with a nail file, and noticed as I did so that round the lid there was a layer of transparent sticky tape. That had been there so long it took a deal of prising off, and I was glad I'd got the job done before we left the house.

"Coming?"

Larry jumped to his feet. "Swings?"

"No. Somewhere different."

I hid the casket in a shopping bag and we drove into town. I left the car in the same car park that I used for work. It wasn't far to walk, and Larry was in good enough spirits to make a go of it without the stroller. Still, when we walked under the bridge, the gloom of the place doused even his chatter. He clasped my hand more tightly as we waited until the only other person on the path had passed with a nod.

On any other occasion under an arch like that I would have taken the chance to show Larry how to set off glorious echoes. Instead, I leaned him up against the brickwork and told him quietly, "Stand very still now. I'll only be a moment. Don't come any nearer the edge."

He watched with interest as I tugged the casket out of the shopping bag and tipped the lid back to let the ashes slide into the dark water. There wasn't time to stand and think deep grieving thoughts. There's nothing like a heap of strangely delicate pale scree to bring it home to you that someone won't return. And right beside me was a child just the right age to catch sight of something curious and wander off without a word, close to the edge.

The last few gritty bits fell in the water. I turned the casket the right way up again, and flipped the lid shut.

"Ready?"

I put out my hand to take Larry's. It was a horrid place and horrid way to let my Malachy go. Still, it seemed right. And anyway, it was a private matter. Together Larry and I walked back along the path. I stuffed the casket and the shopping bag into the first bin we passed, and once again I felt the same old bitter, ineradicable regret that everything to do with Malachy had always ended up working itself out in this drab, seemingly unloving way.

Still, I consoled myself again, no one would know. I would tell no one. Ever.

That is what I thought.

CHAPTER
NINETEEN

And so the autumn darkened into winter as Janie Gay and I fell into a sort of rhythm. Hearing poor Larry howl, I'd sidle out to check the washing on my line. "You're certainly having a hard time of it today!"

She'd hitch her tarty skirt up with her thumbs. "Too right! You'd think the little bastard knows I have a headache!"

I'd lard on my concerned look. "Shall I take him for a while?"

It wasn't in her to be gracious. "I suppose you'd better. If he keeps up this noise, I'm going to slap his bloody face into next Tuesday."

I'd hide my wince. She'd heave Larry over the fence and I would carry him off, still howling horribly. It didn't usually take long to work out whether some toy that squeaked or rattled or parped had just been snatched away from him, or if his meltdown stemmed from hunger or from his mother carelessly cramming him into some garment so scratchy and uncomfortable he couldn't bear it.

I did what I could to solve each problem as it came along and make his life a little easier, even at home. "Hope you don't mind, Janie Gay. He got a bit wet and so I've swapped that checked shirt of his for an old sweater of Sandy's." I might have added, "And given him a glass of milk. And tempted him with a banana. And kept up the pretence that vitamins are sweeties. And given him a bath and washed his hair and sung the little mite some nursery songs instead of yelling at him." The prosecution lawyer at my trial took off on more than one sarcastic flight about my "sanctimonious" claim to have done such a good job of pulling the little boy's life into some sort of order, bringing him regular hours of security and a lot of happy moments. But I believe that it was true. Over the months the tell-tale pallor of the ill-fed child gradually vanished. The little legs grew sturdier. I watched him grow in confidence, learning to *ask* for what he wanted instead of starting to wail, and moving on from simply pointing at objects and animals and saying their names to telling me things about them.

And then one morning something stupid happened. I'd taken Larry to the park. On the way home, I watched him charging merrily ahead of me along the pavement when up behind us came an untrammelled roar. A motorbike without its silencer. Larry spun round. The look of hope upon his face was terrible to see. His eyes shone, and his arms stretched out as if the only natural result of that great deafening crescendo was to be scooped up in the missing Guy's strong, loving arms.

The grinding din followed its maker around the corner and Larry was left staring down a lifeless street. The little face crumpled in disappointment. How long

140

had Guy been gone? Over a year. On this estate, a host of motorbikes forever roared around. Could it have been only because that morning I happened to be a few steps behind that I had caught the look on Larry's face? And so one question spawned the next. Now I not only had to ask myself just how much happiness does a small child need, but day by day alongside that anxiety burgeoned another. How many hours of security can someone his age do without?

And finally one morning in the office, I cracked and knocked on Trevor Hanley's door. At my request, he went to fetch his father. Then, leaning together side by side against the wall, the two of them politely heard me out.

The old man thought at first he must have missed the drift of my proposal. Settling himself in his son's swivel chair, he steepled his fingers and peered at me in rather a worried fashion, as if he feared his failure to understand might be due more to his own ageing faculties than to the sheer effrontery of my request. "I'm sorry, Lois. Explain all that again. You want to *what*, exactly?"

So I went through it one more time, and took good care to add, "It worked very well before, if you remember."

Trevor took up the argument. "But that was just for one week. And you and Audrey and Dana were only working from home because we were putting in the window."

I wasn't giving up. "But I did twice the usual amount of work. You look at the books. You'll see. And I'll come in to the office whenever I can, I promise. Sometimes it might even be for a whole day. And then I won't take lunch hours."

Trevor was looking at me anxiously, as if he'd started fretting on my behalf. Did he think I was crazy? Or was it just his natural kindness showing through? I took the deepest breath. "I'm sure it won't be for long." The next words nearly choked me. "You see, I care so much about my daughter-in-law. And she won't need this extra help for ever. Her little boy will soon be going into nursery."

The elder Mr Hanley jumped on the idea of day care. "What's wrong with him being looked after by someone else now?"

I picked my way carefully through this one. "It's complicated. You see, right at the moment his mother isn't quite herself. She needs someone close at hand to mind him in the house. But because of the state she's in, really it has to be someone she knows. Not a stranger."

I knew I'd won when Trevor began to go over the details again. "And as soon as the child starts at the nursery, you'll drop him off and come straight here, and spend at least those hours in the office?"

"I promise."

"But in the meantime you'll be working from home, but still do a full day's work."

"You know me. As long as I have all the files to hand, I'll probably work even longer hours."

Oh, yes. He knew me. Trevor grinned — a huge broad beam that spread all over his face. "It'll seem very strange without you, Lois. You promise you'll come back as soon as —"

He waited for the name he'd never heard.

"Janie Gay."

"As soon as Janie Gay is over her —" He raised an eyebrow. "What would you call it? Little collapse?"

A picture swept back from the day before. I'd been outside, scraping a teardrop of bird mess off my kitchen window and Janie Gay was sitting on her step, her mobile phone clamped to her ear. Suddenly Larry rushed round the corner of the house, pointing behind him. "Nedgenog! Over there! A nedgenog!"

She'd moved the phone away to spare the person she was talking to, but Larry got it full face. "Shut your face, stupid! Can't you see I'm busy *talking*?"

Even the memory of her tone of voice gave me the shivers. My eyes went round the office. Cream walls and tidy cabinets. A touch of colour in the picture on the wall. Calm. Order. Peace of mind. No way around it. I had come to love this place and all my hours in it.

"Lois?"

I stared at the floor and, when I heard myself answer, realized the person I was trying to comfort was not Trevor Hanley but myself.

"I am afraid I have no choice."

There was a silence, broken finally by an explosion of laughter. I looked up to find Trevor giving me the strangest look, halfway between conspiratorial and stern. "You realize, Lois, that if this outrageous request had come from anyone except yourself . . ."

He left the sentence trailing. And only on the drive back home did it occur to me that perhaps he thought no one except a customer as cool as myself would ever have dared to ask it.

CHAPTER
TWENTY

But I was wrong. Over the next few weeks it became clear there was another motive over and above Trevor Hanley's generosity of spirit. Indeed, the arrangement might have been made to suit him. It must be hard to flirt when at any moment your old dad might sidle quietly past an open office doorway and catch you at it — not to mention the embarrassment of having Audrey and Dana stolidly pretend that they're not noticing what's going on. Small wonder there had been no signs of favouritism up till then. Once I was working from home, his interest in me promptly seemed to ratchet up a gear. Twice I went over to Pickstone to find a message on the answerphone saying that he'd be "passing by" just after work next day, and if I would like him to drop off a fresh batch of files . . .

It made more work for me. I wasn't going to admit I mostly spent my days on Limmerton Road, so I was forced into a deal of extra travel. I'd watch as Trevor glanced around my pretty living room in search of photos that might offer clues to my attachments. He made a point of admiring my tiny arbour so warmly that I was given reason to suppose that he himself had a much bigger garden. He even took the time between visits to look up the names of one or two unfamiliar plants I hadn't managed to track down in any of my own books or catalogues.

Each time he came, he took his time over the coffee. If I had Larry with me, Trevor would watch his antics with that slightly appalled fascination with which those who have never wanted offspring of their own regard small children. If Larry wasn't there, he never rushed to ask the question, "Where's the little man?"

Cheerfully, I'd lie to him. "Off with a little friend. I'm going to pick him up again in just a few minutes."

He'd take the hint, and push his mug away across the table. Once or twice, on his way to the door, he even managed to summon the confidence to try to break through my reserve. "Don't you get lonely, Lois?"

I simply shook my head.

On his next visit he gathered up the nerve to tell me, "The office does seem drab without you."

I looked down at my plain grey blouse and plain grey skirt, and simply chuckled. I think I knew that in some other world, with fewer secrets and responsibilities, I would have taken to this man in the same light and amiable way I'd had my fling with Dan. But this was not the time. I gave him no encouragement, and so the last attempt he made to get the beginnings of a courtship off the ground did take real courage. I watched him fiddling with his spoon for fully a minute before he suddenly raised his head, went red as beet and told me, in a rush, "You do know that if you get bored here working all alone, Lois, all that you have to do is give me a ring and —"

146

I waited. Once again, he lost his nerve. "And Dad and I will come and take you out to lunch somewhere nice. You're not too far from Todmore out here, are you? There's a fine bistro just beyond the racing stables."

I nodded, smiling gratitude, but I said nothing. Horribly disappointed, he gathered the files I'd snatched up from Limmerton Road and stacked on the table so Trevor would assume I'd just been working on them there. I gave him the usual ten-minute start, then picked up the fresh batch he'd brought along and shoved them in a box. Turning the heating down and switching off the lamps, I set off back to Forth Hill, plotting my next attempt to get Janie Gay to "lend" me Larry.

"There's not much difference in height between him and Sandy now. So I was wondering if you'd let me borrow him to test out a couple of second-hand pedal cars down at the thrift shop. If they turn out to be cheap enough, shall I get one for Larry too?"

She scowled. "You want to waste your money on stuff he'll hardly ever use, you go ahead."

Her message firmly sent — "I won't be paying you back" — she'd heave him over the fence. I'm no spring chicken any more and he was getting heavier. And so I seized my chance when once again one day the fast blue car came by to sweep away a spruced-up Janie Gay, and in short order Larry was bundled over to my house.

"I haven't the faintest idea when I'll be back."

"It doesn't matter. You have a good time. Can't have you struggling with a pushchair in that nice top and those shoes."

She smiled. She actually *smiled*. And suddenly she looked so young and pretty. I was still asking myself, "Is this the girl that Malachy and Guy knew?", when out of the car window came her last injunction: "And if he keeps sucking that stupid thumb of his, make sure you slap him. *Hard*."

It made it easy to do what I'd been planning for weeks — go round to her side of the fence and kick at the broken bottom slats until I'd made the hole big enough for Larry to crawl through. Half of the battle. To tempt him, I took to leaving toys he'd never seen before a short way in on my side. Once he was in my garden, it was an easy matter to get him to the back door, then in the house. Sometimes, if Janie Gay was sleeping late, or safely away upstairs in one of the afternoon stupors I took care always to refer to as "Mummy's little naps", the child might be with me for hours, fully absorbed in shunting the little wooden carriages of his train around the edge of a rug, or up on the stool, trying to wrap his chubby hands round mine as I stirred freshly made spaghetti sauce or we made cake dough.

Sooner or later we'd hear that raucous shrieking over the fence. "La-rree! La-rree!"

I'd watch his confidence fade. If he was eating, he'd be off the chair in moments. If we were cuddled on the sofa, he'd slither off my lap. I'd pick up the armful of washing I kept by the door and hurry outside, keeping him safely behind me.

"Larry? He was around the front only a moment ago," I'd tell her. "Playing nicely."

She'd stride off, bellowing that way. "La-*rree*!"

And he'd be safely through, into his own back garden, ready to run round the side of the house and face her irritation.

If I knew there was little chance that he'd be back that day, I would go in to work and face the questions. "How's it going, Lois? Is Janie Gay in any better nick?" There'd be a wistful look on Trevor's face that made it clear he hadn't given up on the idea of getting me not just back in the office, but deeper into his life. If I was not in the mood to face those hopeful brown eyes, I'd choose instead to drive to Pickstone to face the more subtle interrogations that floated over the fence. "Lois! Look at your clematis. It's going *mad*. Shame that you're missing so many days of it . . ."

I didn't want them all to get suspicious. "Isn't it? But I've been spending so much time with my poor daughter-in-law. She's not at all well so I'm helping out a lot with Larry."

"You should have brought the little fellow with you today."

I'd shrug. "Oh, you know. Nice to have the time to do a spot of gardening."

And yet within the hour I'd realize that there might be peace, but never peace of mind. All I was doing was wondering about poor Larry back at Limmerton Road, at the mercy of his mother's foul temper.

Come, come! I'd scold myself. Just how much happiness does a child need to grow and thrive?

But then I'd find myself thinking of Malachy. He'd been years older than Larry and twenty times more canny. Yet when his life became a misery in school time — little more than nine till three — he'd still gone off the rails. So every hour away at Pickstone began to feel less like a break than the betrayal of a helpless child, and as the weeks passed I found I was spending less and less time there.

And I was getting used to the estate. It might be drab, and frighteningly noisy on weekend nights, but always there was something to lift my spirits: rashes of colour in those of the gardens that anyone bothered to tend; the crisp still summer mornings; sunlight on berries, or the first winter rime on walls and fences. Larry and I had merry enough times together and all the time he grew in confidence. Announcements started coming thick and fast. "I'm not scared of spiders and I'm not scared of bats!"

"Good for you, Larry."

"I can walk with my eyes shut!"

I didn't know if he confided the same small proud achievements to his mother. I doubted it. I'd make him supper then I'd take him home. Even as Janie Gay was unbuttoning his jacket she'd already be scolding. "Stand still! Look where you're treading! *Now* look what you've done!" Still, he'd be buoyed with excitement from an encounter with the cat across the way. "I cuddled Harry! Harry let me! And he was purring. Really loud. And then he ran away and we couldn't see him. And Aunty Lo said —"

"Oh, for Christ's sake! You're giving me a headache. Shut your damn hatch!"

The efforts that I had to make never to slap her! Never to tell her what a shrew she was to think her poor child's only role in life was to take on the chin whatever it was she felt like dishing out.

Or keeping from him. One glorious summer morning, I tried to tempt her. "I've a good idea. Let's take my car and go off to the sea."

"I don't like water."

It wasn't said as a confession, more as a statement of pride. I'd very easily become accustomed to Janie Gay's blinkered assumption that anything she didn't care to do wasn't worth doing. (It mirrored perfectly the attitudes of both my bull-necked father and my censorious husband.) But I did think that in this case I might just manage to persuade her into a smidgeon of self-sacrifice. After all, every child has to see the sea some time, and Larry was now getting on for three. I would be doing a favour, not just to him but to myself, if I could teach her how to be a better mother.

So I persisted. "Larry could paddle. You could hold his hand."

"You're joking! Make a rod for my own back? He'll come home moaning all the time." There was no fondness in her imitation of her son. "'Can we go back to the seaside? Can we? Can we? *When?*' Then he'll find out about the pool behind Marriot's, and it'll be nag, nag, nag about that."

"What's wrong with taking him there?"

"Why should I want to go there? I can't swim."

"But you could learn. They do have classes for adults."

"Why should I bother?"

And that is suddenly how I felt. Why should I even bother to say the words, "For *Larry's* sake, that's why." She'd never grasp the point that he was not just some lump of bad luck that had come her way, even a punishment. He was her *son*. Frankly, I couldn't see how anyone could get through life hampered by such cast-iron self-absorption. But thinking only of oneself is probably the strongest of addictions. She'd have top billing, even if her child was weeping or screaming his head off. Whenever I saw them together she seemed to be snapping at him. "Stop making a pudding in your teacup!" "Oh, shut it, Larry!" "Look at me that way one more time and I'll peel you like a banana!" Why should a child his age be expected to handle the fallout from all her vile moods when I could see the neighbours dive for cover each time that she emerged, irritably blinking, to start her endless shrieking? At first I simply thought that Janie Gay, like any other ranting fool, made the mistake of assuming that since she made a deal more noise than anyone around her, her needs were greater than theirs. But gradually I realized the problem ran far deeper. She was what on the estate they called a headbanger. Some days she simply slopped through — careless and inattentive to her child, but lacking venom. On other days, rage simmered behind every look and under every remark, and she became a walking force field of misery and aggression. At any moment at these times, one felt, the last few flapping shreds that tethered her to reality might fray too far and she would lose her grip, and do something terrible.

And that, I realized, was what was causing all those rushes of compassion I kept on feeling. For, when you thought about it, Janie Gay was little more than a living, breathing example of what a child like Larry might become, left to grow up with no protector. If I am honest, I was little short of grateful that the contortion of her personality made it so easy for me to abandon my pretty little house and spend my days on an estate so cheerless it could make you weep. What sort of rancid childhood could have caused some little girl in pigtails to grow up to become someone whose only satisfactions stemmed from being more irritated, and thinking herself more put upon, than anyone around her? And, more disquietingly, what had kept my own son there through all the screaming matches and the fits of rage? Had Malachy sensed, as I did, that inside this spoiled woman there was a childhood so awful, so destructive, so unmendable that all this nastiness was not her fault?

And so I probed, steadily tossing out my casual questions. "Janie Gay, did you grow up round here?" "Which school were you at?" "Do you have brothers or sisters?" Usually she ignored me, brushing away the questions as if her childhood had been something so dull and unremarkable it wasn't worth her while to take the breath to answer. One day, however, I asked her, "Do you get any help at all from any of your family?"

The floodgates opened. "Shite, no! I wouldn't want it, either. Not from that nest of rats."

And out it all poured, about the mother who had run off for the very last time before Janie Gay was even seven; Dad's eighteen-year-old girlfriend, all secret slaps and spite; the final showdown leading to a year in a children's home, followed by foster families who couldn't deal with the endless bunking off from school, the stealing and tantrums, and Janie Gay's refusals to come home at night. Soon she was in the family way, of course. "And he was a right royal bully. He couldn't *stick* the baby making any fuss."

It didn't sound at all like Malachy. "Really?"

"Oh, yes. A proper bastard. Downright nasty! And all too easy with his fists. Really I had no choice, so I just waited till he was flat out one night, and did a flit."

I was appalled. Who would have thought my son could have sunk so low? "He was so bad you just took off? With Larry?"

"Not Larry, no." She scowled. "And anyway, I didn't *take* the baby." The look on her face flattened to one of pure sanctimony. "I should have, though. I knew Ramon would totally arse up looking after her."

Thank God! An *earlier* lover.

And another child. But, my Christ, what sort of mother was she, that she could have a baby when barely out of school and then abandon it the very same way that she herself had been left? And where was that little girl now? Dead after one small fuss too many in front of the loose-fisted Ramon? Or mercifully safe in care? I kept my mouth shut, not really wanting to know. At times like these, the whole demanding business of living among these totally undisciplined people — halfway to feral sometimes — could prove too taxing.

It was with such relief I saw the post van drawing up outside.

"Parcel for Cartright."

"Me!" I called loudly. And I fled.

CHAPTER
TWENTY-ONE

Ramon. Malachy. Guy. Easy to see how Janie Gay could catch a man's attention. When it was not disfigured with scowls, she had a pretty face. And though the garish and ill-fitting outfits she carried home from shopping trips in town were of the sort to make me shudder, when she was all dolled up she could turn any man's eyes.

Forget Ramon. He sounded like a born brute who would thrive in any atmosphere rife with bad moods and spite. But once her character had revealed itself, why did the other two stay?

Had they felt pity? For Janie Gay was definitely what my Scottish neighbour back on Rosslyn Road always referred to as "a right Mrs Nae Friends". Most of the mothers I've known had stronger ties with other females when they had babies and small children than they'd had back in school. But no young woman ever came up next door's path, either alone or trailing toddlers. So either Janie Gay had skipped all her clinics and parenting classes and given birth in a hedge, or, like the blithe miller in the nursery rhyme I sang for Larry so often ("Again,

Aunty Lo! Again!"), she cared for nobody, no, not she, and nobody cared for her.

From time to time young men would come to her door and chat for a while. Old boyfriends? Unlikely. Drug-dealers? More on the mark. She never let them in. As far as I could tell, apart from the driver of the fast blue car who took her off for the occasional spin, she hadn't had a boyfriend since Guy left. (Guy! The very echo of his name would set me praying for the lad's return, and I would have to make an effort to remind myself that he too was someone's son, and down in Dover there was a woman my age who wouldn't be too grateful for me to wish her easy-going, floppy-haired lad back with this peevish harpy.) I couldn't help but think about him, though. And it was obvious why Guy had made such a fine stab of lasting out through the vicissitudes of life with Janie Gay. He was a natural when it came to kindness, and his affection for Larry had been real and strong. I had seen that the day I made my little visit as Mrs Kuperschmidt.

But what about Malachy? Why had he stayed? Had even a boy as immature as he was somehow already known that all you need to break a chain of family misery is someone in the house prepared to take an interest in a child and treat him gently? The longer I thought about it, the more I wanted to be sure my son had stuck it out with Janie Gay from a sense of loyalty to little Larry — or even from selfishness, simply to keep a roof over his head or save on rent — anything rather than having to face the fact that something in the way that Stuart and I had brought him up had triggered in our son a sense of kinship with someone as clearly starved of love in childhood as Janie Gay.

Yes, starved. And so I made a hundred thousand efforts to offer her the small attentions I thought might buff off some of the corrosion left by a childhood like hers. I took all sorts of tacks. And still the only exchanges I ever managed to have with her took place on her doorstep or mine. If I invited her inside, she didn't even answer or make excuses. She simply acted as if my "Why don't you come in? I could make tea" had not been said aloud. I'd try to start a conversation, but it would beach up almost before it began. It was as if she'd never learned how people talk. As she pushed Larry towards me, I'd ask her amiably, "Doing something nice?"

"I doubt it."

And that was that. She'd slouch away as if she hadn't even realized that it was natural to take the time to chat for a moment or two to someone in whose care you planned to shove your child for several hours. Talk only took off if she had the inclination to use it as a springboard to air self-pity. So, burning with the question that only she could answer, I waited till she'd brought Larry to my house one day, then, nodding after him as he scooted past and vanished into the kitchen, I asked her outright, "I've often wondered, Janie Gay. What about Larry's father?"

She gave the most contemptuous snort. "Oh, him? He's dead."

158

Oh, him? I could have slugged her. That was my son she was dismissing like some freshly swatted wasp. But, wait. She wasn't finished. "He was a real dumb loser."

"Loser?" Though she was moving off towards my gate, I still persisted. "What do you mean?"

"You know." She shrugged. "The sort to buy a telly that never works, or vodka that turns out to be water." In spite of herself, she warmed to the task of trashing my son's memory enough to risk an indiscretion. "Mal was so stupid he nearly got me killed once."

"Really?"

"Yes. He owed this guy an awful lot of money. The guy got mad and thought he'd get his own back."

She gave me a sideways look as if in sudden doubt as to whether it was wise to go on with her story. Perhaps the sight of my frilled blouse and sensible skirt gave her confidence that I wouldn't have the slightest clue what she was on about, because she finished up, "Next time they did a deal, this guy fobbed Mal off with some really cheap stuff." She gave the usual martyred sniff. "Of course, it was me that took the bad hit."

I felt like saying, "Our old friend Wilbur, was it?" but kept a grip. In any case, she'd reached the gate and started cursing at the loop of string I'd recently fixed on it to stop young Larry charging into the road. "Well, see you when I see you."

I gave a nod, as if her careless words had been the grateful thanks for looking after her son that had been due. But inside I was thinking just how much trouble would have been saved for me and everybody else if that bad hit had come about a little earlier, and been a whole lot worse.

A few days later, emptying a new batch of files out of my car, I found myself glancing towards Janie Gay's house as usual.

That glint.

Was it her doorkey sticking out from the lock? Well, if it was, here was an opportunity I wasn't going to miss. Hoping that no one on the street could tell from a glance that I was walking as lightly as possible, I went up her path. I had no fears at all about being seen to pull the key from the lock. After all, saving your next-door neighbour from any sharp-eyed ne'er-do-well is only sense.

But one must at least knock. So, raising my hand, I shook it vigorously in front of the door. That would look right.

When, after a while, I still heard nothing from inside except for Larry's howls and the persistent snarls of irritation that passed in Janie Gay's book for "standing firm", I slid away, back to my car.

Her total lack of interest in those around her had always left her blind to other people's altered routines. None of her swathes of grimy netting twitched as I pulled out from the kerb again so shortly after arriving. So off I drove, into the early evening and down to Marriot's, where, in a booth tucked away beside the entrance, two men whose backs seemed permanently turned against the customers spent their days heeling shoes and cutting keys. The girl behind the counter picked out a key base in the only colour left, a lurid purple I would not have chosen for myself but liked at once, and passed it back to one of them along with Janie Gay's key and the graceless warning, "Better get on with it. This one's not shopping. She's going to hang around."

In minutes I was driving home again and back at Janie Gay's door. This time I really knocked while, under cover of the noise, I slid the key back in.

The door swung open. "What the *hell*? Oh. *You*."

I pointed. "Just walking by and thought I ought to warn you . . ."

"Oh, right." She tugged the key out. "That's Larry's fault. The little arse-wipe wouldn't come inside. I had to drag him in. Then I forgot about it."

"Easily done."

Yes. Easily done. And though I wasn't sure how I'd so quickly summoned the wits to take my chance when it was offered me, it was with satisfaction and relief I dropped the purple copy of her key into the little flowered china pot that sat so innocently on my shelf.

CHAPTER
TWENTY-TWO

Next time I took the chance to drop in at the office there was no sign of Trevor or his father. I had become so used to one or another of them hearing the tell-tale buzz of the security lock and leaping out to greet me that I stood rather helplessly in the hall. The place seemed colder than usual. Where were the usual cries of welcome? "Lois! You've never finished Alderson & Howatt? What a gem you are!" Or "Dad was just saying how much he hoped you'd pop in before Friday."

Silence.

Then from inside I heard a fruity sniff. I pushed the door. Dana was at her desk, hunched over a cairn of tissues. "Lois! You'd better keep away from me. I'm a sink pit of germs. I really shouldn't be here."

"Where's Audrey?"

"Still off. This is her cold, you know. She had the damn thing first."

"What about the Hanleys?"

"The old man's just gone home. Same thing, I reckon. Trevor keeps popping in and out." She blew her nose again before she added, "I think he was hoping to catch you. Wants a little chat."

I felt the chill of premonition. Clearly this spread of illness round the office had set the Hanleys thinking that mine was an arrangement that couldn't last. I'd obviously have to tackle the business of getting Larry into a nursery if I were going to get back to my workplace without abandoning the child for too long to his mother's care. I stacked more files, wondering if there was any point in phoning Mrs Kuperschmidt to see if there were any strings that she could pull. But when I tried to think how any conversation of that sort might roll along, I could imagine her suspicious tone. "So, Lois. You're still taking a very deep interest in this child . . ."

Didn't want that. Exchanging a few last pleasantries about the virtues of aspirins and hot toddies, I made for the door. "Tell Trevor I'll do what I can to come in tomorrow."

I said it with so little conviction that Dana didn't bother to respond. I drove off in a flurry of anxiety. Was my job on the line? I had a vision of having to choose between my precious house at Pickstone and abandoning Larry. Perhaps I did take far less care than usual to keep to the speed limit. Maybe I did take chances shooting through amber lights along the Forth Hill Road. All I know is, the drive back to the estate took far less time than usual.

Pulling the box from the car, I hurried up the path and stacked the new files on the usual shelf, way above Larry's reach. I pushed my heaps of current paperwork aside to make some room to go through my own affairs just one last time to see if there was any way that I could run to paying for a place for Larry in a private nursery. No doubt it would turn out to be a stretch too far. It was, after all, only a matter of a few months since the two Hanleys had increased all our salaries, and already the costs of running both houses had swallowed up the difference and stretched me to the limit once again. And I would have to fool Larry's mother into thinking the nursery was free. But telling lies to someone who won't benefit from learning the truth is always easy. And being good with figures was my job. I could at least make an attempt to force the columns to balance.

Almost before I started there was a rapping on the door. Sighing, I rose.

Janie Gay.

She had a dangerous look about her and so, instead of stepping back to let her in, I held my ground in the doorway. "Everything all right?"

Oh, she was certainly in fighting trim. For safety's sake, I pulled the door closed behind me as she lurched forward to thrust a shimmering silver-grey jacket towards me. "See that?"

I caught the stench of vomit.

"So?" she snarled. "What do you call that?"

I couldn't think how best to answer. In any case, it would have made no difference. She had kicked off on one of her tirades. "That's *sick*, that is! This jacket is brand new and now it's *ruined*. And it's all your fault! What've you been feeding him?"

"Look, Janie Gay, I —"

"Come on! What kind of crap have you been shoving down his gob?"

"I can assure you —"

If I'd not stepped aside, she would have pushed the stinking material in my face. "*You* fucking get the stain out! You're the big one for laundry — forever out here hanging stuff on the line so you can snoop at my house over the fence. *You* fucking sort it out!"

She spat — she actually spat — in my direction. Then she turned and strode off. She rarely left without a parting shot and so I waited. Sure enough, as she wrenched open my gate, she hurled one last theatrical gobbet of spite in my direction. "And don't think I'll be letting Larry near you until that jacket's back. And looking *perfect*."

I didn't go inside at once. I think I wanted to let her poisonous miasma dissipate before I opened my door. That is the only reason why I saw the head bob up above the hedge.

"Trevor?"

Realizing he'd been rumbled, he rose to his full height and walked along the pavement to come in through the gate. "Sorry."

"How did you find this place?"

"I followed you. I tried to catch you as you left the office. I thought you'd heard me calling, but you just threw yourself into your car. Mine was right there, so I took off after you." He gave his head a rueful shake. "You weren't half belting it, Lois. I was behind you for the first couple of streets and you never even noticed me flashing." He waved a hand behind him.

"I found a parking space just up the street, but couldn't work out which house you were in." All the time he was talking he was busily prising Janie Gay's stinking jacket out from between my fingers. Dropping it next to the tub of flowers on the step, he ran an arm round my shoulders. "Anyway, Lois, that was all most unpleasant. You'd better come with me, at least until she calms down." He shuddered. "Christ, what a woman! I had no idea what you were putting up with. Let's push off quickly, before the crosspatch little madam comes back for second helpings. I know. I'll take you out for a late lunch."

"No, no."

He swivelled me round, a hand on each of my shoulders. All of his previous shyness seemed to have vanished. "Lois, I'm going to have to *insist*. You can't stay here. She might be back at any moment. I know you're doing your best by her but, really, the woman is unhinged. She looked quite fierce. You would be much, much wiser to leave her house entirely until you're sure that she's calmed down." He looked around in the most business-like fashion. "Now, where's the little boy? Is he inside? Should we take him along with us and leave a note?"

With perfect timing from across the fence we heard a crash, a hard slap and a raging howl. And then that unmistakeably grating voice. "I *told* you not to take that sodding thing outside. Now you stay out with it!"

Slam!

166

Trevor looked over the fence. "Hang on. Wasn't that her?" Baffled, he looked back at my door. "But isn't this — ? I mean, if she's in that house, who is living here?"

I sighed. There didn't seem much point in hiding the truth any longer. "This is my house," I said. "I rent it, just to keep an eye on things." And I pushed open the door. "Come in."

Well, after that, of course, I was Saint Lois. Trevor looked round. He saw the black mould trying to make its comeback. He saw the shabby furniture, the curtains that didn't really fit, the adequate but rather nasty bathroom. And he decided that I was a heroine. The first thing he did was promise me another raise and even (in the strictest confidence) an added bonus for keeping up so well with the work. He even offered to lend me all the money I'd need to send Larry safely off to a good nursery for several hours a day. How could I turn that down? It would be the perfect solution to bridge the gap between my conscience and the situation Larry was in. And I knew I'd be able to pay the Hanleys back. Once I was down to only one house, things would be so much easier.

And so I thanked him unreservedly and knuckled down to scour the city till I had tracked down another jacket of the sort that had made Janie Gay fly off the handle. On the way home, I even bought some flowers to take along as well. I wasn't going to make it easy for her to turn my offer down. I made one fortifying cup of tea and then, unwilling to put off the difficult

167

encounter a moment longer, left the mug steaming on the table and went next door.

Opening the door to my knock, she stared, first at the neatly folded pile of shimmering material, then at the bunch of lilies I was carrying.

Her face stayed set.

"Here," I said, thrusting the jacket into her hands. "I've done it. It's as good as new."

She shook it out and peered suspiciously. "It *looks* all right . . ."

I pushed the lilies closer. "And these are for you."

"Why?"

She sounded so horribly suspicious I fled to the safety of a lie. "Oh, I've just had a brilliant year in the garden. Too many, really. So I thought I'd spread them round."

I looked at her blank face. "They will need *water*," I reminded her. And, since she'd clearly never been offered a bunch of flowers in her whole life, "Perhaps you have a vase. Or jug. Even a food jar. Anything will do."

Already, I could tell, it was beginning to sound like too much work. Rather than tackle the problem herself, she let me in the kitchen. There was no sign of Larry.

"Where's the little fellow?"

"Up in his bedroom."

"Playing quietly?"

"No. He's been sent up there. For cheek."

It sounded so old-fashioned. "*Cheek?*"

"You know," she said. "The same old thing. He wouldn't bloody let up."

"You should have sent him round to me." No point in waiting for a better opportunity. "In fact, I was just thinking that maybe Larry would enjoy a little time in nursery."

"Then tough on Larry."

I pulled a smelly pickle jar out from the chaos of the cupboard under the sink and rinsed it. "I'm sure there are grants and things." My own ingratiating tone was sickening me, but I pressed on. "If you like, I could make a couple of phone calls to try to find out if —"

She brushed the offer aside even before I'd finished making it. "Not worth the effort."

There didn't seem to be a pair of scissors anywhere so I broke off the lilies' stems as best I could to get them short enough to stand in the jar without toppling over. "It might be," I persisted. "After all, the benefits people will be on your back pretty soon, surely, nagging you back to work."

"They'll be on a loser there, then."

"Not keen?"

She snorted. "No, fucking well *not* keen."

I kept on primping the lilies. "They can be horribly persistent — cutting your money and all that."

"Not if you're ill."

This was a new one on me. "Are you?"

"I will be if that lot start up. I'll have that pretend one where you can't do anything except loll about." Putting a hand to her forehead, she did a passable imitation of someone in a Victorian melodrama. "Doctor! I feel so *weak*. I only have to try to get out of bed and I'm *exhausted*."

"What if they're not fooled?"

She shrugged. "You say your back's gone out. You can keep that up for years." She sounded almost wistful, as if it might prove difficult to choose between these two inviting possibilities. "Backache is *better* really, because you can always come right again whenever you want to go out."

"How do you *know* all this?"

She looked at me as if I was daft. "Everyone knows it."

I thought about the piles of papers on my table. All those hardworking people, slogging their guts out in order to pay people like me to work out how much they had to hand over in taxes to subsidize idlers like her.

"But wouldn't you be *happier* sending him to nursery?" Turning my back, I parroted a frequent complaint of hers: "At least then he'd be out from under your feet."

"It's only more *work*," she said, as if I were some halfwit who still hadn't grasped the point. "You've got to remember which days he goes. You've got to get up to take him. You've got to drag him there. You've got to go back to fetch him and bring him home again, even if it's raining. And if you're a minute late, you get a bollocking from all those smarmy, po-faced women."

She might as well have said it: "Easier to pack him off to you, or to his bedroom."

I gave the flowers one last shuffle in their jar. But I could think of nothing else to say to try to persuade her. I think she must have misinterpreted my disappointment as unease, because she suddenly added, almost as if to comfort me, "Don't worry, Lois. He will go to *school*."

School. So. A two-year sentence. Seems nothing *now*, of course. Almost a blink. But back then, in the real world, it seemed a horribly long time.

CHAPTER
TWENTY-THREE

The week of germs passed over. I charmed Trevor into a reprieve by taking home two of the messiest files and holding out the hope of a space for Larry next term at the Sunnyside nursery. Meanwhile, in the attempt to give the child a bit of company of his own age, I stayed on the same old treadmill of mother-and-baby mornings ("Yes, I'm his grandmother"), coffee and playtime in the old church hall, and that old standby of the petting farm, where Larry cuddled the rabbits for as long as he was allowed, kept well away from the turkeys, and queued impatiently for his short turn on one of the dull little ponies.

And it was there that, coming round the corner one day towards the tiny mud ring grandly referred to as "the paddock", I felt the little hand clasped in mine tighten. I looked around to see what animal had startled Larry this time, and there, holding the leading rein of one of the Shetland ponies as it plodded dutifully around the ring, I spotted Guy.

It took a moment to think what to do. I couldn't — obviously — be so cruel as to drag Larry away. I couldn't call to Guy. For one thing, he was being paid to pay attention to the little girl clutching the pony's mane, and for another I wasn't supposed to know him. After all, last time we met I'd had red hair and was pretending to be Mrs Kuperschmidt. So in the end I lowered my head and whispered to Larry, "Want another ride?"

Too overwhelmed to speak, he simply nodded. We joined the line, and as we settled ourselves behind a pair of restless boys tugging their mother's jacket, I took the chance to swivel the little wooden sign we'd just walked past around from *Pony Ride Open* to *Sorry! Pony Line Closed*. I kept on wondering what I would do if one of the other helpers came up to take Guy's place. Would I rush after him to push Larry in his path on the unlikely chance that he would recognize this sturdy little fellow for the unsteady toddler he'd left behind? My heart was thumping on poor Larry's behalf. But though his hand grasped mine more and more tightly, in the end all went well. After what seemed an age of waiting, we reached the front of the line and it was Larry's turn to be swept up by those strong arms.

I did what I could to ease the introduction. "There you go, sweetie-pie!" I said as my small charge was swung up on the back of this so patient pony. "A real little horse ride! *Now* we'll have something to tell Janie Gay."

How could a name like that fail to hit home? Guy stared at the child he'd just plonked in the saddle. "My God! Is it Larry?" Without a thought, he scooped him off again and back in his arms. "Larry-boy? Is it really you?"

The child froze, face as taut as a balloon, eyes huge. It was as if he couldn't bring himself to breathe for fear this was some trick and all the hope that had been building up in him would, like a soap bubble, pop into nothing.

Guy held him further away so he could see his face. "You do remember me, don't you?"

And Larry nodded. This time, when Guy crushed him tight, he slid his arms around Guy's neck and buried his face in his shirt. Guy looked at me over the trembling mop of blond hair. "You see, I *know* him," he began explaining. "The thing is that we used to be —" He started over. "What I mean is, for quite a while I was —"

"I know. A sort of dad to him when he was younger."

He peered at me more closely. "Sorry. Do I know you?"

He didn't sound the least bit confident, so I ignored the question. Once again over me had swept the absolute conviction that somewhere in the sheer good nature of this young man lay hope of Larry's deliverance. So I pressed on. "He talks about you all the time," I lied, knowing that Larry wasn't in a state to raise his head and argue. I larded it on in spadefuls. "He thinks of you as his Dada. He thinks that you'll be coming back — or, at the very least, that you'll come round enough to do a few of the old things with him. He talks about races along the street in the pushchair, and sitting on the seat of your motorbike with you saying, 'Brrrrm-brrrrrrm'. He even remembers you warming up his bottles and cuddling him in the big armchair in the kitchen."

Poor Guy looked stricken. "I thought he was so young he would forget in no time."

I tried to soothe him. "You mustn't blame yourself. A lot of people make the same mistake. And anyway, you probably assumed his mum would get in touch if she was worried."

My passing on the blame to Janie Gay had clearly cheered him. Still, I could see it was an effort to ask, "So how *are* things back there?"

I shrugged.

He misinterpreted my rather glum look. "Nothing much changed?"

"The same old problem." Then I took a chance. "The same old solution, too . . ."

"That bloody Wilbur!"

Bingo!

"Ah, well," I told him cheerfully. "At least we've had the luck of bumping into *you*."

And what a difference that turned out to make. Over the next few weeks I learned Guy's timetable backwards. If he was supervising rides, then Larry had to wait in line like everyone else. But once he was up in the saddle, Guy and I would quickly strike a deal.

"Got any time?"

He would already have been studying his watch. "Look, Lois, can you take him off to see the rabbits or something? My break's at noon today. I'll meet you both up at the café."

We'd save a space. When Guy came in, he'd beckon Larry over to the counter to choose the cake that came free with each helper's break. Together they would wander back, Larry already telling Guy about his morning. "It was the *big* one. With the funny tail. And it was *gobbling*."

Guy did the turkey imitation that so amused them both. The three of us would sit around the table, with Larry merrily dispensing crumbs. Gradually I heard Guy's story. After the break with Janie Gay, he'd gone back home to Dover. Another girlfriend he had met down there had finally decided she was too young to settle down, so in a fit of what he now admitted was pure pique, he'd come back north. Somehow he'd managed to wheedle his way into the petting zoo when they were desperate for staff. Now he was hoping to get a reference good enough to find a job with horses.

To my relief, he seemed to have forgotten "Mrs Kuperschmidt". Even when, in an unguarded moment, I let the subject of Larry's check-ups arise, Guy failed to mention the woman with the bouncy red curls who'd once arrived on the doorstep. But then again, why should a lad his age think twice about some woman far too old for him to fancy? After all, Larry and I had tea with him a score of times over those first few weeks, and yet he barely asked me anything at all about my own life. Clearly he had me down for some old neighbour starved of grandchildren who was content to lavish her affection on someone else's child.

I took my time to find out what I wanted to know. The chance would come. Sure enough, while we were sliding our cluttered trays back on the rack one day, Guy nodded over at Larry, still being chased around the room by two little girls in matching frocks, and asked, "So how's his mother?"

"She's all right, I suppose," I said, adding a fairly neutral, "Sometimes I wonder if she isn't a little lonely."

"Her? Lonely?" I was surprised at his apparent depth of bitterness. "Why should Janie Gay be lonely? After all, she can't stand other women and she can't get on with men."

"You and she stuck together quite a while."

He nodded towards Larry. "I reckon that was more for him."

I trod so carefully. "And surely there was someone else before you."

"Mally? Well, he was a fool. Once he got stuck on the gear, old Mally would put up with anything to keep a roof over his head."

I asked it outright. "Was he Larry's father?"

"That's what *she* said."

I asked the question that mattered. "Do you think he's yours?"

"Not really."

"But he might be?"

He shrugged.

"You've never thought of having one of those tests?"

He stared at me in simple astonishment. "No," he said sharply, and turned away. I hurried to mend fences. "Quite right! It makes no difference to how you feel about the boy." Was there some tactful way of skating over the fact that taking a test would also bring in its train the issue of child support? "After all, why look for trouble?"

I was forgiven. He gave me one of his delightful grins, and called to Larry. As we came out of the café, a silver sun slid out from behind a cloud and the wind lifted. Guy glanced at his watch. "I've still got twenty minutes."

So I slipped away, as I so often did now, leaving the pair of them in one another's company. Moments like this gave me the chance to push off by myself down to the meadow, to watch the stream purling through cowslips and feel content, knowing that every single one of these short visits to the petting farm was yet another link forged on the chain that would pin Larry closer to his precious "Dada".

He must have let the word drop once too often. Or, just for once, Janie Gay must have been listening, because one morning as I was loading files into my car I heard her front door open and the scolding begin. "For God's sake, Larry! Forget your stupid Squeezy Owl and shift your arse! She's just about to leave!"

She'd managed to drag him as far as the gate before I could shut the car door. As I unwillingly wound down the window, Janie Gay said in what she no doubt took to be a persuasive way, "Here, Lois! Didn't you say you didn't mind taking him this morning?"

If I had said it, it was news to me. "I was just off to Marriot's," I explained. I looked at Larry and it was obvious that he'd been crying. My heart went out to him as usual. "But I can easily take him along."

She pushed him forward. "Good. Because there's something that I want to do."

She started back to the house then, on an impulse, turned again. "Oh, by the way, what's all this talk of his about him seeing his Dada?"

Again, I looked at Larry. Now his small tear-stained face had taken on that cretinous emptied look with which he generally tried to fend off trouble. I laughed. "It's not really *his* Dada, obviously," I said to Janie Gay. "But, of all the rabbits up there on the petting farm, the one called Dada is the one that Larry likes best." Loosening my seat belt, I leaned out of the window. "That's right, isn't it, Larry? You do like the rabbit called Dada best of all?"

Not giving him a moment in which to ruin things, I pressed on. "Larry spends *ages* cuddling the rabbits — especially Dada. He even saves cake crumbs for him, even though rabbits aren't fond of cake. And he talks to him about *everything*. Dada and he have lots of conversations."

I thought I must have covered everything.

"Oh, yes! And he always kisses Dada goodbye when he's put back in his cage."

At the first mention of rabbits, she had lost interest. "Well, I'm not sure when I'll be back."

"It doesn't matter. He's quite welcome to stay."

"Good."

Larry climbed in the car. I didn't wink at him. What was the point? Only that week I'd heard some millionaire's daughter saying on the radio that she'd assumed that every child in the whole world had their own bodyguard. Children that age take everything for granted. There are a million things that they don't understand. The best that I could hope for was that next time Larry let slip something about his Dada, Janie Gay would just brush him aside as usual. "Oh, stow it, Larry! Who gives a flying toss about your bloody rabbits?"

Yes. Strange to think that was the best I could hope for. But it was.

CHAPTER
TWENTY-FOUR

The phone call came while I was busy picking up the litter hurled over the fence by passing revellers. Back in the kitchen the washing machine was making such a din I never heard the ring, and so came in to the message.

"Oh, hi. Remember me? From Pritchard Sales and Rentals. I'm in the Kenton office now. I showed you round that house in Limmerton Road." There was a little silence as he gathered his senses. "Where you are now, in fact. Well, the thing is, there's been a bit of movement with this property. So I was wondering if —"

The tape had cut him off mid-ramble, so I phoned him back. "This is Lois Cartright."

A baffled silence.

"Ringing you back," I prompted. "From the house in Limmerton Road."

"Oh, right!" I could tell from the sound of the shuffling of paper that he was rooting round his desk for something that might give him a clue as to why he'd phoned me. At last he found it. "Ah, yes! Of course!"

And after that he was coherent enough. Did I remember the story he might have mentioned about the brothers in dispute over the will? Well, that was now settled. The two had come to terms on a division and wanted to sell the house. Was I aware that I was on a lease that offered me just two months' notice? It was the firm's policy never to post a Notice to Quit through the door without getting in touch first — partly in case the tenant found it upsetting (a lot of them were quite old) and partly because the rental side of Pritchard Sales usually had so many excellent similar properties to offer instead. Why, on the books of the Kenton office alone right now there must be over —

I cut him off. "All right, then. I'll come in and look."

"And I'll post out this letter. I have to warn you that it is a legal document and therefore —"

"Yes, yes. I understand. Two full months' notice. From today. And then I must be out."

"Well, it'll be dated from tomorrow, actually. Because, by law —"

I thwarted his amiable quibbling. "See you tomorrow."

I sat and thought. Another move. And there'd no longer be the hole in the fence, the sheer convenience of being only a curse, slap or squawk away from Janie Gay and Larry. Could it be time to draw back? Had I put in enough for him to start to stand on his own feet?

Clearly not. All I had done so far was tempt a little boy out of the shell that would, if he'd been left to cope alone, have hardened enough to protect him. If he'd been stuck with Janie Gay without me to intercede, he would have grown the sort of carapace that hard-faced children get. He would have taught himself to dull all feeling — firstly for himself and then for others. He

182

would have gone the usual route. She would have swiped him round the head and he'd have rid himself of misery by passing the spite along — pulling the wings off flies or stamping on ants. By the time he was twelve, he might well have become the sort to get a kick out of tormenting cats. By fifteen he'd be getting drunk and kicking his enemies into the gutter.

Why make such efforts, go to such great lengths to start a job and then not finish it? If I bailed out now, Larry would be a deal worse off than if I'd never found him. He'd lose his Aunty Lo, his warm safe house next door, and even have to suffer the misery of losing contact with his precious Guy a second time around.

Out of the question. So I obediently showed up next morning at Pritchard Rentals. "What have you got on Limmerton Road? Or off its side streets?"

Nothing.

"Down towards Marriot's?"

Nothing again.

"What about near the flats?"

Oh, there were places there all right. Half the damn street was boarded up. The rest looked like a bombsite. There was no question of leaving the car within half a mile of the place. And I wasn't even sure I would be brave enough to give it a go. Before I was halfway home I'd almost managed to convince myself that I'd reached such an impasse there was no way out. Kidnap Larry? Ridiculous. I'd be tracked down in a week. Suggest to Janie Gay I rented a room in her house? Forget it. We'd be at one another's throats in under an hour. Feeling a thousand years old, I dragged myself out of the car and up the path, only to find Larry already on my doorstep. He was the easy half of things, I found myself thinking, and took the chance to glower across the fence at Janie Gay's house and will it to crumple to a heap of rubble, crushing the real problem inside.

Larry, it seemed, had come with an agenda. "Aunty Lo, I want a little brown dog."

Instantly the image surfaced of some poor desperate puppy getting a kicking from Janie Gay the same way Larry got the wrong side of her tongue.

"I wonder what your mum will think of *that* idea."

He looked quite baffled. "I mean you and me."

What sort of world is it in which a child can spend so many hours with another person that he assumes he leads a double life?

"I'll have to think about it."

And I did. But not the way that Larry would have wanted. All the suggestion had done was once again bring me up hard against the sense that I was trapped. A dog? Another damn commitment. Another living breathing thing to bring me worry. I was still thinking about the idea when Janie Gay turned up at my door, brandishing a card sent by the Child Health Clinic.

"You'll take him, won't you, Lois?"

"When's the appointment?"

"At three."

"This afternoon?"

She turned a little sullen. "I meant to ask you but I kept forgetting."

Usually I wouldn't have said no. I quite enjoyed these little interviews with the plump lady doctor and her bag of tricks. "So, Larry, can you be a clever boy and point to the yellow bead? . . . Can you throw me the ball? . . . I'm just going to peep in your mouth for a moment." The little boxes on her chart were ticked off one by one. She'd flick back through her notes. "Mother's still working full-time, then?" I'd roll my eyes as if to say, "These girls! What can you do?" She'd tactfully disguise her sympathy for me as a farewell to Larry. "Now you be good to your Granny because she's definitely good to you."

This time, on impulse, I told Janie Gay, "I'm sorry. I can't take him." If she'd been anyone else, I might have pointed to the tax files heaped on my table and muttered something about too much work. But Janie Gay was not the sort to think in terms of duties or commitments, and so I said instead, "I've the most shocking toothache and that's the only time this afternoon the dentist can fit me in."

"Sod it!"

She stood there scowling at me for a while, then added sulkily, "Oh, well. I'll skip it."

"Couldn't you simply take him yourself?"

She looked at me as if I were insane. "For God's sake, Lois! It's two whole bus rides and a walk away." She shrugged. "It's their own fault for closing down that other clinic that they had in Beaver Street."

She turned away, scratching abstractedly. A memory stirred of Malachy standing at the top of our stairs in Rosslyn Road, using his bitten nails to shred his upper arms in just the same way, sometimes till they were raw.

Even the most tolerant child-protection officers take a dim view of certain addictions. Was this the chance to gather ammunition?

"Janie Gay —"

Back she turned, on the off-chance. And yes, indeed, there was the greasy, slightly flushed look that I remembered so well. There were the old blue shadows round the eyes.

Instantly I changed tack. "What if I dropped you off?"

She made a face. "No thanks. I'd still have to do that sodding trek all the way home."

Now that suspicion had taken root, I was determined. "Not necessarily. They have a coffee bar. And Larry will be happy with the toys. You could just wait there till I pick you up on my way back."

She glowered at the card, still scratching furiously. Finally she muttered sourly, "Oh, all *right*." I didn't want to rile her, so I suppressed the urge to point out it was me, not her, offering the favour. Besides, that was no longer true. How often do you get the chance to let yourself in someone else's house with total confidence they can't come rushing back? The urge to snoop had been getting stronger and stronger from the day I got that key. It was her absence of routine that held me back. Sometimes she would be out for hours, sometimes for only as long as it might take to buy a packet of cigarettes, or supper in a box. On one or two occasions I'd even driven past her at the bus stop then, within minutes, seen her stomping back up her garden path, clearly too irritated with the short wait to persist with her plans. Only the most fearless trespasser would risk her sheer benighted unpredictability.

But if you didn't have to be brave . . .

At twenty to three she was, unusually, ready to go. The nervousness I felt affected my driving and twice at successive roundabouts I nearly rammed into the back of the same taxi. She didn't notice and we reached the clinic safe and sound. To keep her happy, I slid Larry a handful of coins while she was watching. "Here you are. This is for you to buy you and Mummy a cake."

He looked a little anxious as I drove off, but I felt worse. Suppose some neighbour saw me? Suppose some passer-by reported back? And yet it was a chance not to be missed, and less than twenty minutes later I had carried a chair out of my kitchen and used it to climb the fence. Inching along the shadow of her wall, I checked to see that no one was about, then scuttled round the front to slip the purple key into her lock. The door swung open at a push and I stepped in that dark dank hall. It took real self-control not to pick up the bags of rubbish she'd left lying there and take them out to the bin. Just *looking*, Lois, I kept having to remind myself. Hands *off*.

I started with the front room. I'd been in often enough when I'd brought Larry home. Always, then, I had made a point of tipping the sleeping child promptly on to the sofa and hadn't risked rousing Janie Gay's temper by staring nosily around. The carpet, I now noticed, was laid in strips, making it clear that, like my own next door, it must have been bought as off-cuts. Where anyone else would have a sideboard or a cabinet, she had a heap of boxes. The greying nets that kept out prying eyes were bunched over the rail in fistfuls rather than pinned or hung. The only pictures were a pencilled view of Notre Dame and a cartoon of a cat. Both looked to me so unlike any choice she might have made that I assumed they must have been abandoned by the last tenant. The room had always struck me as grubby and cheerless, and now I realized one more reason why. There was a fireplace, but it was clearly never used because the heavy chair in front of it faced back into the room. The only splashes of colour came from the heaps of Larry's toys spread on the carpet and across the sofa.

I'd never yet been up the stairs. Usually when my eye fell on all the shreds of tissue and the scraps of toast trailing from top to bottom, I itched to fetch a dustpan. On this occasion they were not too bad; she must have done some cleaning. I didn't have to pick my way round little messes as I climbed.

To the right was the bathroom. She must, I reckoned, have cleaned that too, because it was passable. The towels were thin and nasty — the sort most people keep only to dry a dog. And yet the bath was clean enough. Most of the shampoo bottles on the tiled windowsill had their tops screwed on, and apart from a couple of sodden flannels on the floor — and that was probably Larry — it was quite tidy.

I moved on to Larry's room. I knew it must be his because, disquietingly, there was a proper lock on the outside. How often was that used? With gathering unease I pushed the door and stared around. It was so *bleak.* For one thing, perhaps because it overlooked the garden, she hadn't bothered with curtains. The place seemed chilly enough simply to look at, but it was obvious it would be freezing in winter. His bed looked cheap but adequate, with only its pillowcase of snapping sharks to make me frown: fine fuel for nightmares. I tried to cheer myself on Larry's behalf. At least both of the bright framed posters I had sent around the previous Christmas were up on the wall.

Still, something was wrong.

It took a moment to work out what the problem was. No toys. No books. No jigsaws. Nothing. And when I thought about what I had seen downstairs, I realized that all the bright and cheerful toy cars and games and cuddly animals I'd ever sent him home with ("Tell Mummy Sandy doesn't want it any more") were down in the front room. Had she just finished some ferocious tidy up? Oh, no. I didn't think so. Inside the cupboard there were only clothes. Inside the drawer, just socks. There was a shelf, but it was too high on the wall. No child could reach up there. Only when I had fetched the chair from the hall and climbed on top could I see the things she'd thrown up there: key rings from the pizza house, a broken torch, a plastic banana with chewed ends —

And Malachy's old prism.

The glass was dull with dust and fingerprints. No doubt she'd torn it down in one of her fits of temper. "I'll stop you staring at rainbows! Get those socks on right now!" She'd hurled it up here where the poor boy couldn't reach it as just one more of her spontaneous vendettas against the tiny comforts of someone else's childhood.

Mean-minded little bitch.

I wasn't going to leave the prism there. It held too many memories, and it was doing Larry no good out of sight. I didn't feel the slightest guilt, only a rush of anger at Janie Gay's sheer nastiness, and shame at my own unimaginative failure to realize just how hard her heart could be. How often had I heard her threatening poor Larry with being marched upstairs? But who would ever have thought she'd find the discipline inside herself to make sure that same bedroom could always double as a punishment cell?

And so to her room. What I wanted was a big surprise. What I was longing for, I realized, was to step into such a different world that it would make her guilty, guilty, guilty in everyone's eyes. I wanted to find some warm and comfortable nest that made it plain that here was a mother who knew exactly what she was denying her son. A room so pretty and cared for that it would justify my growing anger and set me free to accuse her: "Look at you! You leave your boy for hours in that cheerless dump you call his bedroom, and yet in here you have soft pillows, gentle lamps and thick lined curtains. You've left your son to fend for himself in that cold cell but you've created for yourself a cosy haven!"

That is what I wanted. A simple black and white scenario to banish the exhausting shades of grey that sent the compass of my feelings forever swivelling to and fro — pity to hate, and back again to pity. But Janie Gay, it seemed, was not one of those mothers who

190

make a palace for themselves and banish their children to an outhouse. Her room was just as bleak. A bed. Drab, serviceable bedclothes. An ugly wardrobe and a couple of pictures on the wall no one her age would choose.

Only one corner of her room would catch your eye — the bedside table. The thing was nothing in itself, small, cheap and chipped. But set on a saucer next to the overflowing ashtray there was a candle. And, next to that, something the shape of a hedgehog made out of strange little wires.

Some sort of lamp? I pressed my toe down on the switch set in the grubby skirting board. Almost at once the spine ends lit up in a glorious metallic blue and, as I watched, melted mesmerically to green, then silver, then to pink, and on and on, through all the colours, clean and beautiful.

I peered in the table's little drawer. My life with Malachy had taught me more than enough to recognize what I saw there: Janie Gay's own small hoard of magic spells. Here was the place she went to throw off all her miseries and disappointments. The only place, perhaps, where it was possible to push away all thoughts of her own childhood, and how things had gone wrong, and how she'd ended up tethered to a responsibility she'd never sought even before she'd had a stab at making something of her own life.

I thought back to the dozens of times I'd wanted to slap her. The times I'd caught her teasing Larry for things he couldn't do, or couldn't quite get out in words. The time she found him lying like a starfish on the floor and said to him, "Dead, are you? Good! Now I can flush you down the toilet where you belong!" The times she caught him wriggling with excitement and cooled his spirits with a sharp "Grubs in your bum?"

And yet again the needle of the compass of my feelings spun, making me dizzy. I felt like weeping. What sort of childhood leaves a young woman like Janie Gay with nothing to console her but her own spite? What sort of empty days were these that could be turned by a few pretty lights into a wonderland?

Poor girl. She'd more excuses for all her pitiful stabs at escape than ever Malachy could have claimed. She'd probably done her best. In future, I would be kinder — renew my efforts to take this pitiful and needy child, as well as Larry, under my wing. The first thing to do was find her some decent sheets, a better pillowcase, a warmer, prettier bedspread. I looked round the room more closely. If I could make some changes in Janie Gay's life, maybe it would be easier to —

That's when I noticed it: a little run of pencil marks along the grimy paintwork as if, when the phone rang, she'd had no paper near and thought it so important not to miss the number she was being told that she had written it on the wall.

And there beside it was a larger scribble.

I bent to take a closer look. No, not a scribble. One small tell-tale letter, carelessly written.

W.

So. Wilbur again.

CHAPTER
TWENTY-FIVE

Early next morning, as I sat in my dressing gown putting in a couple of hours' work, I heard footsteps outside and looked up to see a man's face in the window. My curious visitor was even more startled to notice me than I'd been to see him. Panicking, he pushed his hair back. He was a nice-looking man, my age or a little younger. "God! I'm so sorry! I must have scared you half to death."

I opened the window further. "Can I help?"

"This is so *rude* of me. But, honestly, the only reason that I'm sneaking round like this is that I thought it was far too early to ring the doorbell."

I glanced at the clock. It was three minutes to seven. "Yes," I agreed. "Far, far too early."

He grinned. And, since I couldn't help it, I smiled back. The penny dropped. "You must be one of the old man's sons." I gave him a good long stare, trying to guess if he was the generous brother who'd bought the house for his father, or the unscrupulous schemer who'd held up the division of the spoils till he had wangled a share. But his embarrassed look could have stemmed equally from modesty or guilt, and so I broke the silence. "Come to look at your inheritance?"

I could tell from his face that he hoped I was teasing. So. Probably the schemer. He took a moment to rally. "It's not as if I haven't seen the place before. But this house holds a lot of memories."

"Do you want to come in and look around?"

"You wouldn't mind?"

"No, not at all."

We introduced ourselves. While George was wandering about, I made some coffee. Even before he joined me in the kitchen, he was shouting his patronizing praises from each room in turn. "I like what you've done here, Lois! . . . This is a whole lot brighter than I remember it."

Suddenly from the back bedroom came an apparently sincere, "My gosh, that tree has grown!"

No cherry tree shoots up that fast. So he was almost certainly the more neglectful son. When he came down, this cheerful prodigal took it upon himself to push down the plunger and pour out the coffee even before I had offered it. "I wonder why my parents never thought of moving into the bedroom that overlooks the garden."

I didn't see why I should let the fellow get off scot-free. "Your father did end up there. But that was only because of the shocking damp. By the time I moved in, that front room was a shambles."

He gave a little boyish grin as if the message it sent — "All right, you've got my number. I wasn't the most caring son" — would charm me out of any disapproval. He'd picked the wrong morning for that. After my secret tour of Larry's home, I wasn't in the mood to let off those who didn't shoulder their responsibilities. I simply stared, and in the end he shifted uneasily and tried to defend himself. "Dad wasn't easy to help. He'd hide the fact things needed doing for as long as possible."

"He couldn't possibly have hidden that damp."

George blinked, then bolstered his defence with details I could only suspect him of gleaning from his more generous-spirited brother. "He hated having workmen in the house. He'd lead you into thinking repairs were in hand. 'I've someone coming in early next week.' 'They say they're waiting for a dry spell.' That sort of thing is hard to argue against with an old person."

"Yes," I said drily. "It's never easy to deal with people who twist the facts round just to suit themselves."

Again, that boyish and seductive "so spank me" grin. And suddenly I realized that this man fancied me. Admittedly, I looked my very best. Hoping to keep Trevor sweet on our arrangement, I'd slid into the habit of making more of an effort with my hair on days I thought I might find time to call in at the office. And since my visitor had shown up early, he'd caught me floating round in the silk robe I'd bought for my Italian holiday. He couldn't work me out, though, that was obvious. The question bothering him might have been written in huge black letters right across his face. Why is this woman stubbornly resisting my confidence and charm? Twice before, when he'd walked past the table, he'd raised an eyebrow at the piles of files. Now, shifting the spotlight off himself till he felt safer, he asked me outright. "So, Lois. What's all this?"

"Tax files. I'm an accountant."

"Accountant? What, a *real* one?"

"Any other sort?"

"What I mean is —"

I knew exactly what he meant. Why had a woman with a proper salary chosen to rent this house? I took a mischievous pleasure in giving the honest answer: "I've a close relative along the street who needs a good deal of care."

Astonishingly, instead of looking mortified at yet another dig at his own failings, he took this as a chance to crank up the flirting. "Oh, God, Lois! Don't tell me that. Now I shall feel so terrible you're having to move that I'll have to offer you dinner."

I left him to get out of this as best he could. But he persisted. "Oh, come on. I'm around till Wednesday. How about tonight?"

"Sorry. Salsa class," I lied as coolly as he'd lied to me.

"Tomorrow?"

"Advanced Italian."

"God, Lois! You don't make things easy." But he was giving me a smile that would have made a sphinx grin back. "Look." He reached in his jacket pocket. "Here's my card. You phone me any time and I'll drop all my other plans."

"I'll certainly give it some thought."

He shook my hand in that warm, intimate, double-clasped way. "And thanks so much for letting me look round the old house."

"It was a pleasure," I said.

Because it had been. Watching this smug, complacent stranger oozing out charm had done the best job of reminding me of all the things I truly valued and the sort of man I could respect. And my good-looking visitor had done even more than that. Like one of those bright dancing rainbows tossed out by Malachy's prism, he'd scattered cheering reminders of a freer life. A life I wouldn't have again for quite a while but that might be, *must* be, on its way.

"No, really," I told George again. "It was a pleasure. I'm really glad you came. You were a good start to the day."

Better than what came after. As I was getting in my car I heard the howls begin, and Janie Gay's attack. "Foul little jerk! You did that on purpose, just so I'd have to clean you up. Well, I'm not going to bother. You can just sit in your own disgusting mess all day. Filthy, stupid boy!"

The door slammed shut behind him. He didn't dare sit on the step and spread whatever was in his pants, so he just stood. His cheeks were pink with distress. He'd thrown up a chubby arm to hide his streaming eyes and it was squashing his pretty little nose flat as a button mushroom. I could have folded my arms over the steering wheel, laid down my head and *wept*. For this was not my job. I wasn't paid to save the children of the world from their inadequate mothers. Oh, Mrs Kuperschmidt could spout the official line — imply that things had to be truly terrible before it was right for her and her sort to step in and intervene. But a mere forkful of brain could tell you this was a policy born only of empty coffers. Not enough money in the pot? Then not enough care. For all the dozens of phone calls that filtered in from people worried about the way that things were going in the house next door, how many children ended up with close attention? Four, maybe? Five at the most. So, if the rest of us were not prepared to harden our hearts and keep on pretending, like Mrs Kuperschmidt, that things were "not quite bad enough", then the problems of children like Larry would forever remain problems for people like me. Look at the mite now, standing utterly abandoned on his own doorstep. A little accident. A bit of mess in his pants. Big deal! You'd think from the demented shrieks that had accompanied his ousting that Larry had at the very least smothered a baby, or spread kerosene all round the house and then set fire to it. What was the *matter* with the woman? Why did she have to go into hysterics over the slightest thing?

The child had still not moved. And I was paralysed as well. While he was standing there, feeling so trapped and forlorn, I couldn't drive away. All *right*, I finally snapped at myself. Do something else. Get out of the car, go back inside the house and give it one more try. Phone Mrs Kuperschmidt.

But, really, what would be the point? Already I could hear the conversation we would have. "So, Lois, you don't think the boy's in any actual *danger*?" "Not by your standards, I suppose." "Nobody's beating him?" "I suppose not." "And he gets regular meals?" "Thanks to my efforts." "I take it the house is not in any state we could term 'squalid'?" "No. Not quite squalid enough for your lot. Pity about that." "And it does seem he's doing fine in all his clinic check-ups." "No thanks to Janie Gay."

But that was not the point, of course. What does it matter who looks after a child? The only thing that counts is how that child turns out. And Larry was turning out all right — perhaps not quite the confident, happy child he could have been, but still all right.

The problem was that I was turning too. Turning resentful. Just those few minutes with George had brought back such a flash of the old Lois. The Lois who had so successfully climbed out of the box of her marriage and built a new life. The Lois, indeed, who had spent hours cheerily flirting with her own reflection in hesitant Italian. The Lois who'd spun through her salsa classes with a will, and wept with laughter when her lump of clay shot off the potter's wheel into her neighbour's lap. That laid-aside, but not-forgotten Lois.

The trouble is, you act a part too long and you will almost certainly become that person. George might have come across me with freshly washed hair not yet twisted up in a roll, wearing the bright loose gown I'd bought so cheerfully in another life. But if I looked at myself with more dispassion, I could see that two years of exile in Limmerton Road had turned me into someone else entirely — someone so dull and dependable and middle-aged. A doormat of a woman.

Sighing, I climbed out of the car and called to Larry. The poor lamb didn't even pull his arm from his face as he stumbled blindly towards me.

"Hi, Buster. Time for a change?" I asked him gently.

He was hiccuping back his sobs so violently he couldn't answer. What did it matter? As I led him up the path I realized it was to myself that I had posed the question.

Time for a change?

CHAPTER
TWENTY-SIX

A point brought home when Trevor caught me next day coming into the hall. "Ah, Lois . . ."

Just from the way he said my name I knew he'd come to some decision. I thought fast. "Oh, good! You're here! I wanted you to be the first to hear that I'll be back. Very soon."

I'd really hoped to fob him off with this half-promise, but he still looked anxious. "Very soon?"

Better face facts. "Has something come up?"

He pawed the ground. "The thing is, Lois, that what with Dana going into hospital next month —"

News to me. But rather than remind him of just how detached from the office I'd become, I simply nodded.

"And the fact that she'll be gone for quite a while —"

I kept the act up. "Well, it's quite a business."

He lowered his voice. "The thing is, Lois . . ." Waving me backwards into the privacy of his small room, he picked up more confidently. "I'm not sure she'll be wanting to come back. And even if she does, it'll be weeks."

The way he said "weeks" made it clear that he meant months. He turned towards the window. "I'll be blunt,

Lois. As you'll have realized, we're getting busier all the time. So much work's coming in and we've been barely stumbling through for long enough." He turned to face me. "Dad never likes to change things, but I've decided."

"Decided?"

"We need a proper office manager. I wanted you. If you'd been —" He picked his words with care. "If you'd been fully available, I would have offered you the job. Audrey's not up to it. She would admit that herself." He spread his hands. "But as things are, I fear I'm going to have to bring in someone from outside, and Dad is not at all sure —"

Hugely embarrassed, he stared at the floor as once again he searched for the most delicate way of putting the problem. "Not sure they're going to feel as happy as we do dealing with someone who has to spend quite so much time out of the office."

So that was it. Come back at once, or face the sack.

I made the decision instantly. "Early next month, you say?"

His head shot up. "So, when you told me 'soon' . . .?"

"Yes. I meant *that* soon." I forced myself to sound entirely confident. "Things are more settled on the home front. We've had to take a lot of big decisions. It's all taken time. But I think things are set up nicely now."

He clearly hadn't forgotten Janie Gay. "Really? You honestly believe that poor child will be able to manage without you there?"

"Oh, yes. I think so." I beamed. "And if I'm honest, Trevor, I've really missed the office. You. And your father. I shall be so delighted to be back, and if, as you say, you're looking for someone to take on a few special duties —"

"No, it's a proper step up, Lois. Office manager."

"I think I'm up for it."

"Dad and I agreed you would be excellent." He gave me one last worried frown. "So when could we expect you back full-time?"

What had he said? That Dana was going into hospital early next month?

"Well," I said briskly. "Obviously Dana and I will need a couple of days at least for a smooth handover. So how about a week on Monday?"

His face lit up. "You're sure? I can tell Dad?"

I nodded. I could almost smell my bridges burning behind me, but I still nodded. Then I was in a bear hug. I do believe that, if I'd given Trevor half a chance, the dear man would have kissed me simply from his delight at slipping out of the responsibility of sending me packing. I can't imagine how on earth I thought I might keep my promise. Perhaps in the back of my mind I thought it possible I might persuade some other neighbour with an ounce of heart to take on Larry. Guy didn't come to mind till I was driving home. But once that idea hatched, it seemed to me there was no other possibility. I couldn't wait to get to the petting zoo and track my victim down.

We were in luck. It was Larry who spotted him tipping some grainy grey foodstuff out of a sack into the llamas' trough. I called, and Guy turned, pushing back his mop of hair.

"We need to talk," I told him.

Did he look guilty? Certainly he couldn't turn back to the llamas fast enough. "I'll meet you up there," he said in such a shifty way I almost expected to sit in the cafeteria for an hour or so, and then come out to find he'd vanished. In fact, he joined us only a few minutes later. But you could tell his mind was somewhere else as he went through the old routine of sharing his cake with Larry ("You get this crumb, and I get all the rest. Right?" "Not fair!"), and he was obviously relieved when I suggested we should take a walk down to the turkeys so Larry could once again show us how brave he had become near those unpleasant birds.

As Larry charged ahead, Guy finally made his confession. "Lois, I have to tell you. I've applied for a job."

"A *real* job?"

"Yes."

So much for the idea of him becoming Larry's saviour. My heart sank. "What, with proper horses? Like you had before?"

"That's right. At Todmore."

"The racing stables?" That at least was a relief. It wasn't back down south. But it was still no use to me.

Guy saw my face. "I'm sorry, Lois. I wasn't out there looking. But somebody here happened to mention me to one of the people there — you know, about my old job. And then this phone call came in just a couple of hours ago — Can I get there by three? — and I thought, it's what I always wanted. So why not?" The guilty and distracted look was back in force. "Except, of course, it's going to be a whole lot harder to —"

He tipped his head towards Larry.

I'd only just chosen my own job over the welfare of the child. How could I try to make this boy feel bad? "No, no. You must do what is right for *you*."

He kicked morosely at the gravel path. "They probably won't want me anyway."

"Well, we must hope they do," I told him virtuously, and kept the show up all through the visit to the turkeys, writing his current address down "just in case", encouraging and praising until the moment when he had to leave. As he strode off towards the gates, I even told him again, "I really hope that it works out and you get the job." But after that I couldn't wait to leave. It took a while to drag an excited Larry away from the pen that held the newborn baby chicks, but it could not have been more than a quarter of an hour before, crossing the car park, I noticed Guy at the bus stop, hopping impatiently from one foot to the other.

A car swept past, but not before I'd seen Guy stick out a thumb to try to stop it. Hastily strapping Larry in his seat, I took no notice of the arrows telling me which way to leave the car park, and cruised up behind him. I wound down the window. "What's happened to the bike?"

"Buggered. I've just been trying to start the bloody thing and sod all happens."

His cheeks were burning. He was clearly close to tears of frustration.

"Hop in," I said. "We'll take you."

Out came a little flash of petulance, Malachy-style. "No point. I'd cut it fine in any case, to see those bloody turkeys. We'll never make it."

"Just get in, Guy."

Given the circumstances, anyone else would have climbed in the front. But even at a time like this, Guy took the place by Larry. "Hey, fella! How come you get that comfy seat with straps and I just get to sit on this old boring flat bit?" All the way there, they played some stupid little slapping-hands game while I drove fast. He'd panicked quite unnecessarily. By ten to three we'd reached the stable entrance. A wrinkled ancient in a sentry box took his time finding Guy's name on a list, then put a tick beside it and pressed the gate switch.

"Good security." Guy nodded so proprietorially I knew that in his dreams he was already wearing the stables' dark-green livery. "Some of the racers here are worth the earth."

We were waved through. A long, long shady drive finally spilled us out in sunlight. In front lay a wide stable block with elegant white-painted trim. Behind it was another and, for all we could see, there were more behind that.

Guy stared, appalled. "Jesus! I knew the place was huge. But . . ."

I pointed to a leafy glade that bore the sign *Visitors' Parking*. "We'll meet you there."

Guy hurried off, and I took Larry round the other way to look for horses. Security stayed tight. Twice I was challenged in that urbane, "Can I help you?"

206

fashion, and had to explain our presence. I asked the third man who stopped us, "Would it be better if we waited in the car?" and he denied it. Still, after we'd taken a moment to admire a couple more of those noble nodding heads, I thought it wiser to steer Larry back.

A shortcut lay between two low-roofed buildings.

"Lolo, look! Ducks!"

Larry was right, so we went closer, towards the slope down to a little pond. Just as we reached the corner, I heard a rising babble. A door behind us opened and several children Larry's age rushed out to the play equipment in a fenced yard.

Swings. Sandpit. Tricycles. A climbing frame. Even a little merry-go-round with three painted horses.

Forlornly, Larry stood and watched. After a moment, the young woman supervising this outdoor playtime happened to turn. "Oh, hi! You've come to have a look? I'll let you in."

Better not, I was thinking to myself. Best to explain. But already she was reaching for the safety bar. The gate swung open. It did occur to me that Guy might be another half an hour, or even more. So I changed tack and tried to look as if it were a sensible decision for someone who had brought a young man to an interview to spend her time checking the creche arrangements on the site.

Holding my hand more tightly, Larry allowed himself to be led forward.

"Safe fence," I said approvingly.

"We're very strict about it. Toddlers and duckponds don't mix any more than children and horses." She hunkered down to Larry. "It's nice to meet you. What's your name, sweetie-pie?"

"Larry," I told her, since he clearly wasn't up to it.

She nodded, keeping her eye on Larry. "And do Mummy and Daddy work here?"

There are some things it isn't worth explaining. "His dada might. With luck."

Larry paid no attention. His eyes were following the one empty horse on the small merry-go-round.

"Fancy a ride?"

He nodded, and she took his hand and led him over. "You hang on tight," she warned, lifting him into place. "Georgie can push quite fast." She turned to the small mite in pigtails who had been running round and round, holding the bar. "Now take it easy, Georgie, till you're sure he's safe."

She turned to me. "Go on," she told me. "Go inside and take a look. Even without the children in the room you'll see the sort of place we're running here. So take your time. I'll keep an eye on Larry."

I went in.

This is the moment, said the Prosecution, when I decided. When I looked round that lovely light and airy room. That was the moment.

What utter crap! The world is full of pleasant nurseries for children Larry's age. If that had been the lure, I could have buckled down to half a dozen courses of action to get the same result. Remortgaged the house. Persuaded Trevor to lend me a stack of money.

Even changed my job and embarked on a bit of embezzling. All I was thinking about in there among the painting easels and the huge bright toy bins was how nice a place it was. And what an awful shame that my new responsibilities would stop me bringing Larry up here every now and again for just a couple of hours to see his dada and enjoy the nursery.

No. He would have to come full-time on any day we chose, and even so it would mean getting up at dawn. But it would still be worth it if it stopped this child shifting from who he ought to be to someone I could no longer salvage.

And so, of course, I was absorbed in thinking about Malachy when, through the window, I saw Guy making his way to the car park. Hurrying out, I called him over. Clearly there was some knack to lifting the safety bar across the gate, so we spoke over the fence.

"How did it go? Any luck?"

He looked quite rattled. "Well, yes. I suppose so."

"So you're still in the running?"

"Actually, Lo, I think they might have given me the job."

"You *think*?"

He stood, bemused and anxious.

"Guy, what did they *say*?"

"I don't know. All I remember is them finishing up by asking me if I could start on Monday."

"So you *have* got it."

He still looked anguished. "Do you really think so? Maybe they only meant —"

"Oh, nonsense! What else did they talk about? Did they talk money?"

"Yes. I can't remember. But it was more than I get now. *And* I get a place on site."

"What, free?"

"I think so. I *think* they said I get my own shower room but have to share the kitchen with some of the other lads."

"What about the hours?"

"Not brilliant," he admitted. "But then again, I'm sort of on probation. Right now they want me to put in time early in the morning, exercising horses, mucking out and stuff. Then I'm to start again in the late afternoon when all the kids who get to take private lessons pitch up after school."

It sounded rather good to me. "So you'll have quite a block of time off free each day?"

"Except at weekends. Then I'm working solid."

That didn't bother me. I made my pitch. "If I could find some way of getting him here, could you put Larry in this creche?"

For the first time, he looked around him. "*Here?*"

"Why not? It's for employees, isn't it? And you'll be an employee. Larry would enjoy it. And you'd still get to see him."

"Can I afford it?"

"It can't be all that much. And I could help you out."

We stood and watched as Larry gingerly lifted a hand from the bright-yellow mane he'd been clutching so tightly, and then, with growing confidence, waved at us both in triumph.

"Oh, Lois," Guy asked. "Do you really think things might be coming right for me?"

"Why not?" I said, and thought about the countless times that Mrs Kuperschmidt had tried to comfort me by banging on about all the young people she'd known who'd finally pulled together a second chance at life, and thrived again.

We stood together quietly, still watching Larry. It was the exact right moment for the sun to do my bidding — slide out from behind a cloud to catch the coloured rinse I had been mixing, week by week, into the child's shampoo. ("Washes out grey." But could it wash out doubt?)

I had to feel complacent. I had done a brilliant job. The little mop was flashing glints of perfect marmalade.

"He *is* your son," I said to Guy. "How can you even question it? Look at his hair!"

CHAPTER
TWENTY-SEVEN

Only one fly in the ointment. Janie Gay. She lost her temper. "Fucking well nothing to do with you!"

"He needs a bit of company."

"Oh, bog off home. It's not your business."

"I know. But I just happened to come across the place. And it is perfect. He could sleep over at my house once or twice a week and I could drive him out there early, before I go to work, and pick him up after. It would give you a break." I took a risk. "After all, he does spend an awful lot of time with me anyhow."

"He fucking well does not!"

I backed off hastily. "Well, you know. Quite a bit. And I thought you'd be keen on the idea."

"Well, you thought *wrong*."

I did a bit of grovelling in her doorway, and then I vanished. Give her a couple of days, I thought. Leave her to deal with her own son without a break and she'd soon change her tune. I took the chance to spend a couple of days away in Pickstone, and helped Guy move his few possessions into his room in Stablelads' House. I didn't mention what had happened back at Limmerton Road when I'd suggested the creche. The lad was nervous enough about his new job. I didn't want to add another worry. Each time he asked me, "Do you really think that she'll let Larry come to nursery all the way up here?" I waved away his concern. "Of course she will. I just have to pick the right moment to ask her."

And I suppose things might have worked out that way in the end. They *might*. But something happened to throw me off the primrose path of patience. I'd reasons enough to want things settled. After all, in fewer than ten days I was supposed to be back in the office full-time. My rented house would be swept out from under me a fortnight after that. And when she saw the two of us carrying Guy's boxes across the courtyard, the nice young woman from the creche had called us over. "There's only one place left until I get more staff. Shall I keep that for Larry?"

But I can swear that it was something else that tipped the balance. It was the afternoon that Janie Gay finally cracked — almost a whole week later — and dragged Larry to my door. "*You* take the little shit. He's been an arse all day. He's lucky that I haven't killed him. You claim to like him so much. *You* sodding have him!"

And off she stormed. I led him to the armchair and washed his maggot-white face. I made him toasted cheese — his favourite food — and let him watch cartoons until his painful hiccups stopped.

I switched the television off. "Coming to talk to me?"

He shook his head. I gave him a brief reassuring cuddle and left him in the armchair with Squeezy Owl, an engine and some books. Quietly I went back to work. Usually Larry found the rustle of my papers so soothing that often I'd lift my head from inputting some firm's accounts to find he'd fallen asleep. On that particular afternoon I just pressed on, thinking I'd work a little longer before I took him off to bathe the sticky salt of tears out of his hair. Sometimes, as he sat in the deep warm water, building foam castles out of the bubbles I'd whipped up as a treat, he would begin to talk about whatever it was that started the fuss. "The light was off and I couldn't turn the handle," or "Wilbur was stamping on Squeezy Owl, and she was laughing." He was so quiet sitting in the armchair, it was a while before I realized what he was doing. He'd pushed the books aside and picked up the battered advent calender I had been given by one of our clients a couple of Christmases before, and which he loved. For what seemed to be the thousandth time, the child was opening and closing the little windows on the coloured card.

Whispering.

Suddenly suspicious, I slid back from the table and moved as quietly as I could till I was right behind. What was he saying? Even as I leaned over to listen, Larry was prising another window open to peer at the picture beneath.

"*My* house."

I waited, barely breathing, as with his little thumb and finger he clumsily lifted the next flap. "*My* pussy." Then the next. "*My* toys."

Creeping around, I tried to read his face. Could it be wonder? After a year or more of his devoted fingerings,

214

could that old battered card still seem to him a magical swirl of glittering bright colours?

Not wonder, no. I watched that child laying his finger on the cosy fireside, the shining presents heaped up on the hearth, the steaming cups, the plump, contented cat curled on the cushion, and had to turn away. It seemed for just a moment so intolerable that someone his age — too young by far to give a jot for any calendar festivity — could be so obviously consumed with longing.

For that was what was on his face. Longing. Here was a boy who, if he could, would crawl inside a tattered advent calendar to be in that safe, cheery room.

Christ knows, a simple enough wish. A happy home.

I blew my nose. I gave the child his bath. I took him back and told the usual lies to Janie Gay. Larry was "sorry". I thought he might be coming down with a fever. He was very hot. That would excuse his behaviour. He had the sense to keep his eyes closed and she let me carry him up the stairs, into his bedroom. I shook the ghastly shark-ridden coverlet more warmly over him, whispered goodnight and shut the door behind me.

Safely back home, I started work again. But something was wrong. No matter how many times I ran the figures, the columns on the screen refused to come right. Simply to clear my head, I pulled a sheet of paper towards me and drew a line as usual down the middle, from top to bottom.

And that is how it happened, I suppose. Something to do with thinking in debits and credits. The credit side filled up nicely. Poor Larry would be so much happier. The new responsibility would settle Guy for life (though he would have to get rid of the motorbike; I would insist on that). I could go back to the office. And back to Pickstone. Larry could come to me at weekends when Guy was working all hours. Larry would love the nursery. And no one on the street would ever have to hear that awful woman screeching "Larr-eee!" ever again.

And on the debit side?

I sat there, sucking my pencil. If I am scrupulously honest, I couldn't think of a thing. Even when I successfully dredged up some airy-fairy reason like "She is a human being," I'd find my pencil drifting to the other side and see I'd written down some counter-argument along the very same theme: "One fewer scrounger off the state." (I had the decency to cross that out.)

So there it lay — the most telling of indictments: a neatly written list of all the reasons why the world would be a better place if Janie Gay were gone. A weight of misery and irritation and other people's efforts that could be all so easily expunged.

And on the other side — nothing. A total blank. This is the point, of course, at which the rest of the world falls back on all those lofty Thou Shalt Nots sprinkled from heaven. People are quick enough to drop their hypocrisy as soon as the deed is done. "I can't say I'm sorry he's gone." "No great loss there." "Bit of a blessing all round, if you want my opinion." But still they'd baulk if, two or three days earlier, you'd asked them to pitch in and help with the solution.

No. I knew I'd be on my own.

So I chose Saturday 29 November. (No point in hanging about.) I bought a sheaf of gift vouchers from one of the shops that Janie Gay could never pass without a wistful scowl. "Too sodding posh for me. I couldn't even afford a pair of their socks."

Not daring to doctor the vouchers, I put them in a separate shiny envelope on which I printed "Expiry date: 30 November". I took them round. "Look what I found at the bottom of a drawer."

She pulled the vouchers out of the envelope and fanned them through. "Bully for you!" she said sourly.

"I thought you might want to use them."

She gave me a suspicious look. But in her scheme of things, of course, I was still trying to crawl my way back into her good books after our little tiff about the nursery. I saw her weighing her response almost as carefully as I'd weighed up the problem. On the one hand, the pleasure of shoving the vouchers back in my face. And on the other —

"All right. I'll take them."

She flicked through once again, checking that the amount was what she'd thought and made the bargain worthwhile. And clearly even Janie Gay could not disguise the fact that she was pleased because she said, "Thanks, Lois."

"*Thanks, Lois*"? This is, perhaps, what Mrs Kuperschmidt is getting at when she suggests that I should think about the choices I made. After all, this was the very first thank-you that I had ever had from Janie Gay. Should I have tried to build on it? To see it as a ray of hope, a stepping stone to improvement, a portent of a better future for every single one of us?

Oh, yes! And we'd have all grown beards down to our feet waiting for paradise. "Now," I reminded her. "Just don't forget the shop doesn't open on Sunday so I'm afraid today's the very last day that you can use them."

I waited.

Sure enough, her next words were: "You'll have to look after Larry."

So I did. And I got busy. First I settled him in front of a film I knew he loved so much he couldn't put on Pause. I clattered round the kitchen to give him the impression that I was still about, then took the purple key and slid next door. I'm not a star on wires in a house, but it would take an idiot not to be able to find a place behind the furniture where someone's phone line can be razored in two. Neatly I mopped up the almost invisible flakes of skirting-board paint with a damp finger, and pushed the cupboard back in place.

That was the landline done and I went home. The mobile was a different matter and would take cunning. I kept watch from my window until I saw her tottering up her path, swinging her shopping, and made sure only a couple of minutes had passed before I was back round there with rather a sullen Larry snatched up from some absorbing game with Squeezy Owl.

I showed the greatest interest in the glossy bags piled on the kitchen armchair. "Can I peep?"

The nearest she could come to gratitude was an ungracious "I suppose so". I didn't let her rudeness rattle me. I picked the first package out and shook off the pretty pink tissue. "Oh, that is *lovely*. You'll look *splendid* in that." I kept it up, praising the slinky dress, the low-cut tops, the vulgar shining belt, until I reached the last of her choices. "Oh, look at this! Cut on the bias. It must hang like a *dream*."

She shrugged.

"Oh, go on. Show me. Put it on."

Smart to have picked the skirt. If I had handed her the dress, she would have balked. Far too much effort. A skirt was different. All that she had to do was hop from one foot to the other, keeping her balance, while she peeled off her jeans. Then she pulled on the skirt and struggled for a moment with the zip.

And that is all the time it took to slide her mobile phone out of the bag she'd left on her kitchen counter and put it in my pocket. I admired the skirt. (She did look good, I admit.) And then I turned to go as she swung open the freezer door and stared inside.

"What's Larry like with mushrooms?"

Shopping with other people's money is clearly hungry work. Even before she'd finished the question, she'd made up her mind.

"Oh, who cares? Mushrooms is what I feel like. If Larry's going to be a fusspot he can pick his off and trade them for my crusts."

Why did she always manage to make it so very easy for me to steel my heart? I kept my hand on the door.

"Oh, yes," I said. "I very nearly forgot. This bloke was hanging round outside your gate. I told him you were out. He said he really needed to see you, but not at his flat. You weren't to ring him either. He was a bit cagey, but I had the feeling he thought there might be something fishy about his phone line."

Now she was staring. "Something fishy? You mean, like being tapped by the police?"

I shrugged.

I'd made her anxious, I could tell. "What did he look like? Did he tell you his name?"

"No. But it was obvious he was in a state. And he kept saying he had something for you. Something important. But he could only keep it till tonight."

"Tonight?"

"He just kept rattling on about needing to meet you under some bridge near Ballantyne Street car park."

"That stone bridge over the canal?"

"How should I know?"

I watched her look down at the pretty skirt. She even twitched her hips from side to side to make it swirl a little. Spending an afternoon flouncing about in a dress shop had probably reminded her of life outside. *And* it was Saturday night. I watched her make her mind up. "You can take Larry, can't you?"

I'd thought about this. Sometimes in life it's best to take a back-row seat.

"Sorry," I told her firmly. "Out myself tonight." Lowering my voice as if I didn't want the child in the next room to hear, I added, "And if you want my opinion, Janie Gay, you'll stay well away yourself. He seemed to me to be a very creepy type. To tell the truth, I was in two minds about telling you." I leaned towards her confidentially. "I even think he might have been on *drugs*."

CHAPTER
TWENTY-EIGHT

So, when you think about it, it was Janie Gay's decision to slip out to try to find her precious Wilbur. "Here is a case in point," says Mrs Kuperschmidt each time the subject of that evening comes up. "There was a child of three left unattended in the house. That is illegal. All that you had to do was phone the police. Within an hour, that child would have been out of there. Your worries could have been over. Janie Gay would have been cautioned, and social services would have been on the case."

And what sort of farce would that have been? Poor old Joe Taxpayer forking out more hard-earned cash for yet another flurry of investigations and case interviews, all ending up with some soft magistrate offering a dolled-up Janie Gay "just one more chance" and sending a gullible social worker round once a month to get fooled by a pack of lies. No. I was the one with the problem and that was not a plan I had much time for.

Better to settle it now and settle it properly. So I'll admit I did ignore the fact that Larry was left home alone while I locked up my own house and hurried along to where I had discreetly parked the car a few hours earlier, two streets away. For quite a while I must

222

have been behind the very same bus that Janie Gay took into town, and would have overtaken it but for the fact that I had to pull off into that video-store car park to tug on the red wig.

It smelled a little musty, which I thought odd considering I'd kept it in the box in which it came, and it had cost so much. It still looked good though, giving me confidence that, what with the tightly belted raincoat that Janie Gay had never seen me wearing, she wouldn't recognize the person coming her way until it was too late.

Ballantyne Street car park was closed. That didn't bother me. I found a space on the next street and even had the presence of mind to drive to the end and back, so I'd be facing the right way when it was time to go home. I locked the car, tightened the belt on the raincoat, and set off walking briskly towards the bridge, lowering my umbrella to shield my face whenever anyone walked past.

Saturday night. In spite of the weather there were a good few early-evening revellers. It worried me. I knew the streets could only get busier. But all of them were headed off the other way, towards the city lights, and by the time I reached the bus stop nearest the bridge, no one was about. I'd cut things very fine, I realized, because far down the street — so far away I only noticed when she stepped under a streetlamp — I caught a glimpse of Janie Gay already making her way around the corner of one of the narrow interlocking streets between the road and the canal. I set off after her. It was a bit like playing Grandmother's Footsteps.

At first I thought she might suspect that she was being followed, but after a bit I realized that every time she heard a noise or saw a moving shadow, she stopped to peer about her, hoping, no doubt, that it was Wilbur. So we made crab-like progress down the street, with me continually flattening myself into the dark of doorways. I was as sure as I could be that if she suddenly swung around and saw me in the full glare of a streetlight, I would still seem as much a stranger to her as I had to my father during Malachy's funeral.

Still. Best to be careful.

It was a whole lot easier along the towpath. The place was full of shadows. Frankly, I would have thought it safer to put a fence along and keep it locked at night. I wouldn't say that I was frightened, exactly. And it may sound perverse, but every time I heard the scurry of some small creature my footsteps had disturbed, or strangely shaped bushes loomed at me suddenly out of the dark, I was quite glad that Janie Gay was there.

We reached the big wide sign behind which I'd once stood watching her so reluctantly offer a drag of her cigarette to my besotted son. ("*Oh, him.*") And as she picked her way along the path from there towards the bridge, I had the feeling everything was running backwards, and if I could just get her under that arch where I'd first heard her shrieking her insults at Malachy, I might be able to stop time in its tracks — make it unravel in a different way.

And now she'd stopped. We were so close, but she'd no wish to go in that dark place for no good reason.

Restlessly she stood about, occasionally going nearer the bridge mouth to peer inside.

She wouldn't wait for ever. No one was coming along, so I climbed up the bank on to the roadside. I don't think she can have heard my footsteps as I walked past above her. Only one car went by, and that was going so fast I almost fled for fear that the police would almost certainly be chasing it. Once on the far side of the bridge I slithered down to reach the other black and gaping mouth.

Then I called to her. "Hey! Janie Gay? That you?" I made my voice sound rough. She wouldn't for a moment think this was a man shouting through the arched space. But with the billowing echo — "you . . . you . . . you . . ." — she might confuse my voice with any one of all the other druggies she must have met at Wilbur's place and it might give her confidence she wasn't alone on the towpath.

Her voice was tentative. "Hello? Who *is* that?"

I answered even while her echo rang. "Down here," I called. "We're all down here . . . here . . . here . . ."

That was enough. She moved under the bridge. I saw her only as a blacker shadow coming towards me.

She didn't see me at all.

"Oof!"

That's what she said as she fell in the water — "Oof!" — just like some character in a cartoon. I stepped towards the edge but barely had a moment in which to see in the slick of light thrown by some passing headlights her look of pure astonishment before her coat sucked up enough of the water to start to drag her down a second time. She opened her mouth. To call for help? Abuse me? I still think, from the way she looked at me, it might have been to ask the simple question, "*Why?*"

And that was that. Once her mouth filled with water, the poor girl didn't stand a chance. The struggling went on for quite a while, but was a losing battle. Even if I had wanted to pull her out, by then I couldn't have reached her. She'd flailed her way too far from the brick side.

I watched the oil-black water suck her down and along. By the time she'd safely vanished we had moved out from underneath the arch and were a good few paces along the path. I could have praised her timing. People were coming along the towpath towards us. Quickly I slipped behind the bushes till the little gang of them had wandered past. Then, putting up a hand to check the wig was still on properly, I hurried back to where I'd parked the car and I drove home.

It was a bit of a restless night. For one thing I was worried about poor Larry. What would he think when he woke up to find his mother gone? I knew I mustn't go next door too early. It would look odd. The whole street knew she was no early riser. Painful as it was, I had to wait.

But it was the police who showed up first, with all their questions. Had I seen my neighbour from next door?

"Who? Janie Gay?"

When was the very last time that I had seen her? Please think carefully. Guesses aren't helpful.

Of course I knew exactly. "Half past six last night. I took her son home. I'd been babysitting him at my house while she went shopping."

That's all it took. "So you do know the little boy? He's confident with you?"

"Oh, yes. I spend a lot of time with Larry. And since his mother has no car, I'm usually the one who takes him off to see his dad."

He was a kind man, that was evident. His face lit up. "Oh, so the boy is still in touch with his father?"

"Not just in touch. They're very, very close. In *fact —*"

So it fell out the only sensible way. Instead of whipping Larry off to strangers in a temporary foster home, they brought him round to me. Guy was a suspect for only as long as it took the seven other stable lads to pool their photos of him acting silly on his first night out. So it was only a few days before I was allowed to take Larry to Todmore. And there (after all the cuddling and a few rides on that delightful painted horse) it was the work of a moment to agree the best course of action.

And that's how things worked out. *Perfectly.* I was delighted to get back into the office — and to my house in Pickstone, where Larry settled in as easily as if he'd never had another home. I only had to go back once, for Squeezy Owl. (She'd thrown him up on the high shelf as some sort of punishment, and when I finally found him there after a good bit of searching I felt a stab of joy that I had rid the world of such a nasty piece of work as Janie Gay.) Once he had Squeezy Owl, Larry fell easily into the pattern we'd arranged for him. I woke him early so I could drop him off at the creche and still get into work before Audrey. Guy sprung him for an early lunch, then took him back to Stablelads' House for a shared nap before the afternoon session. It was a long day for a little boy. Nonetheless, when I came by to pick him up after work, it was often quite hard to prise him off the merry-go-round, or out of the wooden "castle". So by the time that social services finally came round to give us the official nod, we were all revelling in our new lives.

Perhaps too deeply. Now, I look back and almost can't help being amused to think that Joshua Omulolo found that slip of paper with the neatly pencilled list on it on the exact same day that Trevor Hanley asked me to marry him.

"Why me?" I'd asked. "I thought I was supposed to be too cool a customer for you."

Trevor had gone bright red, and done his usual trick of pawing the carpet like a guilty twelve-year-old. "Oh, well. You know."

"No. I don't know."

He seized my hands. In his great paws, they felt like little birds. "Yes, you do, Lois. Please don't muck about. We've wasted so much time already. Just say yes to me. You know that we'll be happy."

I did, too, thanks to the recent visit from that smug charmer George. So I said yes. Now everyone was happy. Obviously I couldn't share the thought with Trevor or his father, but I did feel as if some gloriously technicoloured play had worked its way through to the final act. Everything had fallen out perfectly and all of us were at last revelling in our just deserts.

And then the phone call came.

Trevor and I were in bed. "I won't take that," he offered, but as his arm was already reaching out towards the bedside table I thought I might as well be gracious. "No, no. Perhaps you'd better."

Relieved, he put the phone up to his ear. "Hi, Dad."

I suppose I knew the call concerned me just from the way that Trevor shifted the phone from that ear to the other. One moment I could hear the chirruping of Mr Hanley's voice, the next I couldn't. Though Trevor didn't seem to move away from me in bed, I felt a distance, and Trevor himself spoke only in monosyllables. "Yes . . . Now . . . No." Oh, and the care he took not to let his eyes slide round to meet mine! I knew it was bad.

Indeed it was. A barely credible run of rotten luck when you consider that just one tiny thing falling out differently could have stopped the disaster in its tracks. If Ainsley Forsyth plc hadn't been suspected of minor VAT fraud and had their files marked up for special attention by one of the department's auditors. If Joshua Omulolo had only been a little busier that day and actually worked through lunch instead of idly picking up that stupid list of credits and debits that fell out of the file in front of him while he was eating his sandwich at his desk, and idly wondering what it could mean. But then again, if Mrs Omulolo had not been five months pregnant, her husband might not have been keeping his eyes peeled for prospective names. And if Janie Gay's mother and I had had the sense to call our children by names a little less striking, then Joshua Omulolo's attention might not have been drawn to the article in the paper that made such a big deal of the fact that Malachy Henderson's wife Janie Gay had drowned in the very same canal as her husband, and on the anniversary of his death.

All very striking.

Without that sheet of paper (neatly entitled "J.G. — Pros and Cons" — what *was* I thinking of?) I would have definitely been home and dry.

But as it was, the game was over.

CHAPTER
TWENTY-NINE

"Five minutes," the police officer had said, and made it clear she meant it by standing stolidly in my bedroom doorway while I was gathering the few things I'd need. Seizing a moment when she turned her back to answer a shout from downstairs, I tugged down Malachy's glass prism — hung in the window only a few weeks before to sprinkle dazzling rainbow promises of peace and happiness around the room.

A fitting seal on things, I'd thought, to show the world was back in place.

When we came downstairs, Trevor was standing watching. I asked the officer, "Mind if I give him a hug?"

"Don't make a meal of it," she warned, and didn't see me dropping the prism in his pocket. I knew he'd keep it safe. He kissed me briefly on my nose as if I were a child before they took me off. Once at the station, I did my bit to try to shift the blame. "All I know is that she went off to see some bloke called Wilbur."

Naturally they knew the name. Out of a sense of covering all bases, they put a tail on him, and snapped up more than enough evidence within a week to feel obliged to charge him. I couldn't help but feel some satisfaction — a second bird killed with my little stone? — but in the end it proved small comfort. The way of the world is such that Wilbur's drug-dealing was judged so petty — and dealt with so fast — that he was out again before my own trial. (I saw him sneering from the gallery, and when my sentence was announced, the man had the nerve to whistle his approval.)

I wasn't going to confess. Doodling a list of pros and cons for someone's death does not make you a killer. Still, thanks to Stuart's all too successful disappearance all those years ago, suspicion mounted. Information filtered in. (Even that bloody wig-maker woman remembered my face.) There are more cameras about than you would think on streets and in video-store car parks. The evidence stacked up about my visit to the bridge. I argued forcibly enough that people go to visit their children's graves. Why shouldn't I have chosen the anniversary of his death to go back to grieve at the place where I'd poured my son's ashes? But I was on a losing wicket. Stuart was somehow dug up, and though I don't believe his whole intention was to show my black heart and sheer implacability, he didn't help. "Yes, it was Lois who threw Malachy out on the streets . . . No. That's right. Lois never visited her mother when she was dying . . . Yes. It is true that Lois didn't attend her funeral."

Well, thank you, Stuart. Thank you very much.

During the week in which that bitch of a prosecuting counsel kept flapping that bloody wig in the jurors' faces and letting rip about my capacity for secrecy and my pure cunning, I felt obliged to offer Trevor back the ring he'd given me. "I will admit," he said, "that Dad has spent a good deal of time this week warning me I might regret saying the words 'till death do us part' to a homicidal maniac. But shall we just press on? See how it goes?"

As any fool could see, it wasn't going to go well. And sure enough, after a quite insultingly short time out of the court discussing the matter, the jury trooped back in and they pronounced me guilty.

Trevor was calm enough about the news. "Eight years, my sources suggest. So, Lois, if you behave yourself in clink you might be out in six. Shall we just wait and see? And if you still fancy the idea when you come out and I'm still ploughing this long and lonely furrow . . ."

Frankly, I think he is amused by the idea of marrying a jailbird. "When we get married," he tells me on visits, "you'll have to promise never to take me on any walks near the canal." Once, just as the warder was looking at her watch in that determined fashion, I asked him what his father had to say about his plans and he was decent enough to look me in the eye and tell me outright, "If I am honest, Lois, right from the start, Dad has been far more upset about the fact that my eye fell on someone too old to give me children."

I made a face and shrugged. "We could adopt."

After, when I was in the queue to get my revolting supper, one of the other girls who'd had a visitor that day asked me, "What did you say to set that bloke of yours laughing so hard he nearly fell off his chair?"

"Oh," I said. "Nothing much. We were just talking."

"What about?"

I gave it a little thought. And then I answered, perfectly honestly, "We were just talking about how sometimes in life you can get second chances. And sometimes you can't."

The other brick is Mrs Kuperschmidt. She couldn't be more disapproving if she tried. But all her training leads her to follow guidelines. ("Sarah, your doing that is what fetched me up in here!" as I say bitterly. "So you had damn well better keep it up now!") The rules say Larry's interests must come first, and since I'm definitely the most consistent emotional attachment in Larry's life, she's swung things so he gets regular visits. Guy brings him in. We have a laugh. Larry gets spoiled to death by all the prison officers and volunteers in the creche. I think he likes the prison, and Guy appreciates the fact that having to bring him to such an out-of-the-way spot twice a month means that he gets to use my car.

And Mrs Kuperschmidt was a real gem about my father's death. She knew I couldn't give a toss, but she still sent one of her brilliant read-between-the-lines notes as good as telling me which tack to take in my request letter to the Governor, and also hinting that there would be others present to make the effort worthwhile. So I was granted permission to go to the funeral. Trevor was there. And Guy and Larry. And Sarah herself. Once we'd spilled out into the crematorium grounds, it turned into a party. (No one was going to waste time grieving for that mean-spirited old goat.) It was so lovely to be out under trees, and see green distances instead of gates and walls.

I sidled up to Trevor. "Did you bring it?"

"Would I forget my orders?" He reached into his pocket and drew out Malachy's prism. He had polished it until it shone. The small length of invisible fishing wire I had attached to it when Malachy was little now had an added length of silver cord.

I looked around for Larry. As usual, he was mucking about with Guy, playing some jumping game around the graves. I called him over.

"Here." I gave him the prism. "Hold it up, sweetie."

It caught the sun. Larry was staring into it so hard he didn't notice what was happening across his clothes and mine.

"Look at your woolly."

The movement he made in glancing down set rainbows swaying. He stared, entranced. Did he remember it? Did he remember anything? We never asked. He never said. All that was obvious was he was *happy*.

I felt pride bursting out of me and I reached out to set the prism spinning just as Malachy used to do. The sprinkles swayed and danced.

My grandson's eyes met mine. "Is it for me, Lo? Can I keep it?"

"Oh yes. It's yours." I took the little swan-shaped hook I'd made in metalcraft out of my bag and handed it over. "Your dad will hang it for you."

I turned to Guy. "You'll fix it in his bedroom window for him, won't you?"

Guy grinned. "Sure, Lois. Nice for him to have a keepsake from his da —"

He broke off just in time. Not that I think Mrs Kuperschmidt was close enough to hear, or that it might have set Larry thinking. After all, the child is only seven. But there are things best left unsaid and there'll be time enough for all of that when Larry's older. Right now we're all a whole lot safer sticking with a fiction that suits us all.

I think that Sarah Kuperschmidt was quite surprised at my good spirits on the journey back. "Usually, even the tiniest taste of life outside can be unsettling." I won't make the mistake of putting things this way to the parole board, but I did try to explain how I never minded going back inside after these rare trips out because I honestly thought that, though things had turned out strangely, they had turned out well.

"Balanced," I told her. "Almost biblical, in fact. A life for a life."

For I did feel that, through my lack of courage and attention, I'd let one child go to the bad. But then the very Lois who'd emerged from that was the same Lois who had grown the wit and guts to save another. Don't things even out?

She was appalled by the suggestion, I could tell. And so I hastily pretended I hadn't meant it. Just a flash of black wit. I was so sorry. And the moment passed. She's a kind woman or she wouldn't visit me.

And so we made our way towards Security. "Now don't forget," she took the trouble to whisper in my ear before they led me off towards the wing. "Next week, before the parole board. You are *sorry*, right?"

Yeah. Right.

Also available in ISIS Large Print:

Salt

Jeremy Page

Every story heads towards tragedy, given the time.

A man is found buried up to his neck in the thick mud of the Norfolk saltmarshes by a woman gathering samphire. Nine months later, at the end of the Second World War, he vanishes, leaving a newborn daughter, Lil.

Lil's life is singled out from the start as being strange. Taught by her mother to read the clouds, she lives a curious existence on a land so often overrun by the sea. But when, as a teenager, she becomes the object of two brothers' desire, her life begins to spiral out of control.

Forty years later it is Lil's son, Pip, who attempts to makes sense of his family's intriguing history. Will the past repeat itself and is Pip, like his forebears, beginning to lose his own way between the creeks and the samphire?

ISBN 978-0-7531-7994-9 (hb)
ISBN 978-0-7531-7995-6 (pb)

Envy

Judy Corbett

She thought I was her best friend — she had no idea how wrong she was . . .

Isabel is the daughter of the local landowner and lives in the big house, a beauty who basks in love and security and exudes sweetness. Her friend Diane is the daughter of a tenant farmer living in a broken-down cottage. With a distinct lack of life's advantages and bitter memories of childhood, she is not beautiful: she is clever, vengeful and consumed with envy. Their friendship very quickly becomes intense, and Diane is invited to live in the big house.

What happens when your daughter's friend turns out to be a destructive cuckoo in the nest? When girlish charm turns to seduction and teenage friendship to manipulation? How can just one teenage girl wreak such havoc on a decent, loving household?

ISBN 978-0-7531-7902-4 (hb)
ISBN 978-0-7531-7903-1 (pb)

Over

Margaret Forster

A serious pleasure to read   **The Times**

Louise, a mother and primary school teacher, is trying to hold herself together after her teenage daughter dies in mysterious circumstances. She's trying to get on with life, trying to understand not "what happened", but what is happening to them all in the wake of the accident, and why.

Don, her husband, cannot accept that his child's death might have been an accident. He wants someone to blame, becoming obsessive in his quest for a reason, travelling restlessly, neglecting work and family in pursuit of the "truth". Their other children handle the tragedy better than their parents. What they can't deal with is the way their parents are tearing each other and the family apart.

ISBN 978-0-7531-7894-2 (hb)
ISBN 978-0-7531-7895-9 (pb)

Keeping Faith

Jodi Picoult

For the second time in her marriage, Mariah White catches her husband with another woman, and Faith, their seven-year-old daughter, witnesses every painful minute. In the aftermath of a sudden divorce, Mariah struggles with depression and Faith begins to confide in an imaginary friend.

At first, Mariah dismisses these exchanges as a child's imagination. But when Faith starts reciting passages from the Bible, develops stigmata and begins to perform miraculous healings, Mariah wonders if her daughter — a girl with no religious background — might indeed be seeing God. As word spreads and controversy heightens, Mariah and Faith are besieged by believers and disbelievers alike, caught in a media circus that threatens what little stability they have left.

ISBN 978-0-7531-7830-0 (hb)
ISBN 978-0-7531-7831-7 (pb)

Raking the Ashes

Anne Fine

Lovers, colleagues, family — Tilly has always been brilliant at pushing people in and out of her life exactly as it suits her. Then along comes Geoffrey, gentle, compassionate, generous to a fault, with his miserable little children and his manipulative ex-wife.

Tilly's own expertise in the arts of deception and avoidance should be enough to make sure she's always one step ahead of Geoffrey's wretched crumbling family. But time and again she finds herself staying, brought down by their cowardly backsliding and their barefaced lies.

How has she managed to stay so long in a relationship that she knows perfectly well has to be doomed? More importantly, how can Tilly plan her permanent escape?

ISBN 978-0-7531-7403-6 (hb)
ISBN 978-0-7531-7404-3 (pb)

ISIS publish a wide range of books in large print, from fiction to biography. Any suggestions for books you would like to see in large print or audio are always welcome. Please send to the Editorial Department at:

ISIS Publishing Limited
7 Centremead
Osney Mead
Oxford OX2 0ES

A full list of titles is available free of charge from:

Ulverscroft Large Print Books Limited

(UK)
The Green
Bradgate Road, Anstey
Leicester LE7 7FU
Tel: (0116) 236 4325

(Australia)
P.O. Box 314
St Leonards
NSW 1590
Tel: (02) 9436 2622

(USA)
P.O. Box 1230
West Seneca
N.Y. 14224-1230
Tel: (716) 674 4270

(Canada)
P.O. Box 80038
Burlington
Ontario L7L 6B1
Tel: (905) 637 8734

(New Zealand)
P.O. Box 456
Feilding
Tel: (06) 323 6828

Details of **ISIS** complete and unabridged audio books are also available from these offices. Alternatively, contact your local library for details of their collection of **ISIS** large print and unabridged audio books.